SAO SWORD ART ONLINE

003

REKI KAWAHARA   ABEC   BEE-PEE

SWORD ART ONLINE
FAIRY DANCE

"Hurry...Hurry and come save me, Kirito..."

Asuna § A girl held prisoner in the VRMMO ALfheim Online

"Let's hurry! We're off to the World Tree!"

Leafa § A girl who runs across Kirito in ALO. She plays a sylph character.

"You never have a care in the world, do you, Papa?"

Yui § An AI who reveres Kirito as her "Papa." In ALO, she assists him as a Navigation Pixie.

"It's just so…I dunno, *moving*. I wish I could keep flying like this forever…"

Kirito § The mightiest solo player in SAO. In ALO, he plays as a spriggan warrior.

"I'm so stupid, stupid, stupid!"

Suguha Kirigaya § Kirito (Kazuto Kirigaya)'s sister. A kendo fighter in her third year of middle school.

"If you can withstand thirty seconds of my attacks, I will believe that you are an envoy."

Eugene § The strongest warrior in all of fairydom, a salamander. He wields the legendary "Demon Blade Gram".

"Very generous of you."

World Tree

The final destination of all players in ALfheim Online

The first fairy race to reach the legendary floating city atop the massive World Tree and have an audience with the Fairy King Oberon will be reborn as the true race of fairies known as "alfs." Alfs are no longer subject to the game's restrictions on flight, meaning they can fly an infinite distance—the true rulers of the endless expanse of sky. The floating city is reached through the dome at the foot of the World Tree, but the dome's entrance is protected by impossibly powerful guards. In a year of game time, no player has succeeded in that quest as of yet.

SWORD ART ONLINE
FAIRY DANCE

VOLUME 3

Reki Kawahara

abec

bee-pee

YEN ON

NEW YORK

SWORD ART ONLINE 3: Fairy Dance
REKI KAWAHARA

Translation: Stephen Paul

SWORD ART ONLINE
© REKI KAWAHARA 2009
All rights reserved.
Edited by ASCII MEDIA WORKS
First published in Japan in 2009 by
KADOKAWA CORPORATION, Tokyo.
English translation rights arranged with
KADOKAWA CORPORATION, Tokyo,
through Tuttle-Mori Agency, Inc., Tokyo.

English translation © 2014 by Hachette Book Group, Inc.

Yen On
Hachette Book Group
1290 Avenue of the Americas, New York, NY 10104

www.HachetteBookGroup.com
www.YenPress.com

Yen On is an imprint of Hachette Book Group, Inc.
The Yen On name and logo are trademarks of Hachette Book Group, Inc.

First Yen Press Edition: December 2014

ISBN: 978-0-316-29642-7

10 9 8 7 6 5 4 3 2 1

RRD

Printed in the United States of America

"THIS MIGHT BE A GAME, BUT IT'S NOT SOMETHING YOU PLAY."

—Akihiko Kayaba, *Sword Art Online* programmer

SWORD ART ON fairy dance

Reki Kawahara

abec

bee-pee

Three lights, deep blue, arranged like a whispering constellation.

Suguha Kirigaya reached out to trace those lights with her fingertips.

The LEDs on the front rim of the NerveGear VR headgear indicated its current status.

From right to left, they represented power, network connection, and brain interface. If that leftmost light ever switched to red, it meant that the user's brain had been rendered nonfunctioning.

The NerveGear's wearer was resting on a large, soft gel bed in the midst of an off-white hospital room, deep in an un-waking sleep. But no, that wasn't quite right. His soul was actually in a far-off world, battling day and night. Battling to free himself and thousands of other players held prisoner.

"Big brother..." Suguha softly called out to Kazuto. "It's been two years already. I'm going to be in high school soon...If you don't come back to us, I'll shoot past you..."

She dropped her fingers down to trace his cheek. His flesh had sunk over the long course of this comatose state, as though it had been carved out. Kazuto's facial profile was already soft and androgynous to begin with, and now it looked more feminine than ever. Their mother had even jokingly called him "our Sleeping Beauty."

It wasn't just his face that was gaunt; his entire body was painfully thin. Athletic Suguha, who had been actively training in kendo from a young age, almost certainly outweighed him at this point. Lately, she was gripped with the terrible thought that he might just wither away into nothing.

But for the past year, she'd made certain not to cry while in his hospital room with him. Not since she'd heard the news from the member of the Ministry of Internal Affairs team in charge of handling the "SAO Incident." The man with long bangs and black-framed glasses spoke with a note of respect in his voice: Her brother was currently among the very top players within the game when measured by level—one of the capable few pushing the forward progress of the game, despite considerable personal danger.

Even now, he was probably facing death within the other world. Which meant that Suguha couldn't sit here crying over him. She had to take his hand and give him her full support.

"Hang in there...You can do it, big brother."

She clasped Kazuto's bony hand in both of hers, praying fervently, when a voice from behind caught her by surprise.

"Oh, you're already here, Suguha."

She hastily spun around. "M-Mom..."

It was their mother, Midori. The sliding doors on the hospital room were so quiet that she hadn't noticed they were no longer alone.

Midori put the bouquet of cosmos into the vase at the side of the bed and took the seat next to Suguha. She must have come on the commute home from work, as she was wearing a rough leather blouse over a cotton shirt and slim jeans. Her light cosmetics and carelessly tied ponytail did not suggest a woman who would be in her forties next year. She had the energy of a much younger woman, perhaps due to her job as the editor of a tech magazine. Suguha often thought of her more as an elder sister than a mother.

"I'm surprised you had time to visit, Mom. Isn't the print deadline coming up?"

Midori flashed her a grin in response.

"I pushed my way free this one time. I don't usually manage to visit, so I wanted to make time today."

"That's right. Today's his…birthday…"

The two stared in silence at the bed and its sleeping Kazuto. The sunset breeze pushed the curtains and sent the smell of the cosmos wafting under her nose.

"Kazuto's already sixteen," Midori murmured. "I remember it like it was yesterday. Minetaka and I were watching a movie in the living room, and Kazuto snuck up on us and said, 'Tell me about my parents.'"

Suguha saw a brief, nostalgic smile play across her lightly rouged lips.

"He caught me completely by surprise. He was only ten. We were going to keep the secret until you were in high school, Suguha…another seven years. But somehow he realized that certain parts of his citizen record were deleted."

She'd never heard this story before. Suguha's initial reaction was not shock, however, but the same wry smile on her mother's face.

"Geez…that's *so* him."

"He caught us so flat-footed that we weren't able to deny it very convincingly. That must have been by design. Minetaka even agreed that he got us good."

They laughed aloud together, only to return to watching the sleeping Kazuto in silence.

Suguha's brother, Kazuto Kirigaya, had been living with her for as long as she could remember, but in reality he was not her brother—he was her cousin.

Midori and Minetaka Kirigaya were Suguha's parents, but Kazuto was the son of Midori's sister, Suguha's aunt. Kazuto's parents died in a tragic accident when he was not even a year old.

He survived, though with significant injuries. Midori then took in her nephew as her own.

Suguha had only known the truth for the past two years—since the winter after Kazuto had been taken prisoner by the virtual world called Sword Art Online. Already traumatized by the awful circumstances, she turned on her mother, demanding to know why the truth had been kept from her for so long.

Even now, two years later, she still felt a deep, simmering discontent that she'd been the only one excluded from the knowledge. It was only recently that she'd finally begun to understand her parents' line of thinking.

The reason they'd sped up their schedule and told Suguha the truth before she entered high school was a bitter one: They wanted to ensure she knew while Kazuto was still alive. The SAO Incident resulted in an alarming number of deaths—more than two thousand in the first month alone. Under those circumstances, her parents had no choice but to face the very likely possibility that Kazuto would die. They wanted to ensure that Suguha wouldn't regret something she'd never known until it was too late.

Suguha visited Kazuto's hospital room often, searching for some kind of answer, conflicted by an array of clashing emotions. If her brother wasn't really her brother, what was it she was losing?

The answer she arrived at was: nothing.

Nothing was changing. Nothing was damaged or lost. Before and after the truth, Suguha's only course of action was to pray for Kazuto's life and safe return.

Two years later, one of those two prayers was still working.

"Hey, Mom," Suguha said softly, still watching his face.

"Yessum?"

"Do you think that has anything to do…with why he got really into online games right around the time he started middle school?"

She didn't say the stuff about not being a real member of the family, but Midori understood and shook her head immediately.

"No, that had nothing to do with it. He built his own rig from some spare parts I'd left around the place when he was six. Did you know that? If anything, he managed to remotely inherit my computer obsession."

Suguha giggled and elbowed her mother's arm. "Grandma told me once that you were addicted to video games when you were a kid."

"That's right. I was playing games online when I was in elementary school. Kazuto had nothing on me."

They laughed together once again, and Midori cast a loving glance at the figure on the bed.

"But I was never one of the top players in any of the games I played. I didn't have the force of will or patience for it. That's the part he shares with you, not me. Kazuto's alive now because he has the same blood of yours that's kept you in kendo classes for the last eight years. He'll be back one day, mark my words."

Midori patted her daughter on the head and stood up. "I'm going to head on home now. Don't stay too late."

"Don't worry, I won't," she replied.

Midori took another look at Kazuto and murmured, "Happy birthday." After a few rapid blinks, she turned and swiftly left the hospital room.

Suguha placed her hands in her lap, took a deep breath, and stared at the LEDs on the surface of the headgear that covered her brother's head.

The blue stars that represented the network connection and brain status were blinking rapidly. Somewhere beyond that connection, Kazuto's mind was within the world of SAO, sending and receiving countless tiny signals through the NerveGear.

Where was he now? Wandering through a dim dungeon with map in hand? Browsing items at a shop? Or swinging his sword bravely at some horrible monster?

She reached out and held his pale white hand again.

The NerveGear blocked the sensations on Kazuto's actual skin at the spine, and the feelings did not reach his brain. But Suguha believed that the fervent support she sent him through their skin would find its way to him.

She could feel it. Her brother's soul—her *cousin's* soul—was emitting a powerful heat. A sign of absolute will to survive and return to the real world.

The golden light filtering through the white curtains turned to deep red, then purple. The hospital room sank into the gloom of night, but Suguha did not budge. She sat perfectly still, listening to each and every fragile breath her brother took.

She received word from the hospital that Kazuto had awakened one month later, on November 7th, 2024.

1

Clak, clok.

The unfinished rocking chair rattled pleasantly on the porch.

Gentle late-autumn light filtered through the cypress branches. Off the distant lake blew a slight breeze.

She was dozing gently, her cheek resting on my chest. Her breath was slow.

Time passed drip by drip, golden with serenity.

Clak, clok.

As I set the chair to rock, I stroked her soft chestnut hair. Even in her sleep, a faint smile played across her lips.

A few juvenile squirrels frolicked in the front yard. A pot of stew was bubbling back in the kitchen. Life in this tiny house deep in the woods was so tranquil and easy. I wished it would last forever, but I knew it couldn't.

Clak, clok.

With every creak of the rocking chair, another grain of time fell.

I clutched her tighter to my chest, trying to resist that inevitable passage.

My arms embraced nothing but empty air.

My eyes flew open with a start. An instant earlier, our bodies had been touching, but she'd disappeared like a lie. I rose and looked around.

The sunset was growing radically darker moment by moment, as though it were a stage effect in a theater. The creeping night turned the forest black.

I stood up into the wind, blowing colder than before, and called out her name.

There was no answer. She was not in the front yard, now devoid of any critters, nor was she in the kitchen.

Somehow, the house was completely surrounded in darkness now. Like a children's pop-up book, the walls and furniture of the little cabin fell flat against the ground and vanished. Soon, the only things around me were the rocking chair and the night. The chair kept rocking back and forth, without anyone in it.

Clak, clok.

Clak, clok.

I shut my eyes, covered my ears, and screamed her name with every ounce of strength I had.

That scream was so powerful and real that even after I bolted awake, I couldn't be sure if I'd screamed aloud or if it was only in my dream.

I closed my eyes again in the vain hope of returning to that dream's happy beginning, but eventually I had to give up the dark and open my eyes.

It was not the white panels of a hospital room but walls with narrow wooden boards that came into my vision. The bed, too, wasn't made of an advanced gel material, but a mattress with cotton sheets. There were no IV drips stuck into my arms.

This is my— This is Real World *Kazuto Kirigaya*'s bedroom.

I sat up and looked around. The room had authentic wood flooring, a rarity in this day and age. There were only three pieces of furniture: a simple computer desk, a wall rack, and my pipe-frame bed.

The rack was the kind that tilts to lean against the wall. Sitting on the middle shelf was a piece of headgear in a faded navy blue. A NerveGear.

This was the full-dive VR interface that had trapped me in a virtual world against my will for two whole years. It was only after a long and terrible battle that I was released to see, touch, and feel the real world again.

I was back.

But the girl who'd swung her sword at my side, who'd shared her heart with mine...

I squeezed my eyes shut, turning away from the NerveGear, and got to my feet. I looked in the mirror placed on the other side of the bed. The electroluminescent panel embedded in the mirror placed the date and time just above the reflection of my face.

Sunday, January 9th, 2025, 7:15 AM.

Two months had passed since I'd returned to the real world, but I still wasn't used to my appearance. My old form as Kirito the swordsman and my real self, Kazuto Kirigaya, bore the same face. But I still hadn't regained the weight I'd lost, and the bony body beneath my T-shirt was frail.

I noticed in the mirror two shining tear tracks on my cheeks, and I reached up to wipe them away.

"Look at me, Asuna. I'm such a crybaby now."

Muttering, I walked to the south end of the room and the large window there. With both hands, I cast open the curtains and let the wan sun of a winter morning dye the room's insides pale yellow.

—✶—

Suguha Kirigaya strode across the frosty lawn making pleasant crunching sounds.

Yesterday's snow had almost entirely disappeared, but the mid-January morning air was still cold enough to bite.

She stopped at the bank of the pond, frozen over with a thin film of ice, and let the *shinai*—her bamboo kendo sword—rest against the trunk of a black pine. Suguha inhaled deeply to banish the last remnants of sleep from her body, then put her hands on her knees to begin stretching.

She gently, slowly loosened the muscles resisting the call to wake. Toes, Achilles tendons, calves—the blood flowed faster into each in turn, bringing forth telltale prickling.

She put her hands together and stretched them straight down, and when her waist was fully bent over, she stopped dead still. As she arched over the pond, the smooth surface of the morning's fresh ice reflected her figure.

Suguha had cut her hair straight across, just above the eyebrows and the shoulders. It was so black that it almost had a bluish tinge. The ice showed her a girl with brows equally black and thick and large, confident eyes that gave her a boyish air. Particularly when you considered her outfit: an old-fashioned white *dogi* with black *hakama* bottom.

It's true... He and I really don't look alike...

It was a thought that occurred to her often these days. It popped into her head every time she looked in the mirror in a bathroom or the foyer of their house. She didn't hate the way she looked, and she wasn't particularly disposed to caring about such things, but now that her brother, Kazuto, was living at home again, she couldn't help but compare them.

No use thinking about this.

Suguha shook her head and resumed stretching.

When she was finished, she grabbed the bamboo sword off the pine tree. She gripped the old, familiar handle, letting it sink into her hands, and then straightened her back, hands at stomach height.

She held her breath and pose—and, with a sharp cry, swung the blade straight downward. Several sparrows took off from the branches over her head, startled by the disturbance of the morning air.

The Kirigaya home was an old-fashioned Japanese house in the southern region of Saitama Prefecture, a former castle town that still featured many of its archaic sights. Their family line could be traced back many generations, and Suguha's late grandfather, who had died four years ago, was a strict man of the old ways.

He had served on the police force for many years and was said to be quite a kendo practitioner when he was young. He was hoping for the same from his only son—Suguha's father. But her father only swung the *shinai* until high school before transferring to an American college. Once out of school, he went straight to work for a multinational securities company. He met her mother, Midori, after getting a transfer to the Japanese branch, but his work still took him back and forth over the Pacific constantly. As a result, her grandfather's fierce passion was typically directed at herself and Kazuto.

Suguha and her brother were enrolled in a local kendo dojo at the same time they entered elementary school. Kazuto seemed to be influenced more by Midori's job as the editor of a computing magazine—he loved the keyboard more than the sword, and he'd quit within two years. But Suguha, who was only placed in the dojo to keep her brother company, took to kendo quite easily, and she still practiced it now, even after her grandfather was gone.

Suguha was fifteen. Last year, she'd placed among the top in the country at her final middle school kendo meet, and she'd already earned a recommendation to one of the premier schools in the prefecture for kendo.

But…

Suguha had never struggled with her direction in the past. She loved kendo, and it made her happy to please others and meet their expectations.

But ever since the incident that shocked Japan and stole her brother two years ago, a seed of doubt had grown within her, one she could not remove. You might call it regret—regret that she had not tried harder to fill the deep, wide gap that grew between them when Kazuto quit kendo when she was seven.

After leaving kendo behind, her brother had taken to computers as though slaking an unquenchable thirst. As an elementary school student, he'd built his own machine out of spare parts, even doing some rudimentary programming with their mother's guidance. To Suguha, he might as well have been speaking a different language.

Of course, she'd learned how to use a computer at school and even had one of her own in her room, but the most she used it for was e-mail and web browsing. She didn't understand the world her brother lived in. The online RPGs he played were even more baffling. She couldn't fathom ever wanting to wear a mask to hide herself and playing along with other masked people.

When they were much, much younger, Suguha and Kazuto had been closer than friends. But when he'd ventured off to this strange world she didn't understand, Suguha filled that sense of loss and loneliness with kendo. Yet the more she swung her sword, the less they talked and the further apart they grew, until that became the normal state of things.

But deep down, Suguha still felt that loneliness. She wanted to spend more time with her brother. She wanted to understand his world, and she wanted him to see her compete.

Before she could bring herself to talk to him, the Incident had happened.

The game of nightmares, Sword Art Online. The minds of ten thousand young Japanese had been trapped in an electronic prison, asleep to the outside world.

Kazuto had been taken to a large hospital in the city of Saitama. On the first day that Suguha went to see him, surrounded by cords in that hospital bed with the hateful apparatus stuck on his head, she'd cried uncontrollably for the first time in her life. She clung to her brother, wailing and bawling.

She might never talk to him again. Why hadn't she tried to close the distance between them? It shouldn't have been that hard. It should have been possible.

That was when she'd begun reconsidering in earnest her reasons for doing kendo. But no amount of agonized deliberation brought her an answer. She turned fourteen, then fifteen, without her brother. She moved on to high school, following the path others laid out for her, but she never once was certain that she was moving in the right direction.

If he came back, she would talk to him in earnest. She would reveal all her anxieties and indecision and ask for his advice. And two months ago, a miracle had occurred. He broke the shackles of his own accord and came back.

But much had changed between them by this time. Suguha's mother had revealed that Kazuto was not actually her brother but her cousin.

Her father, Minetaka, was an only child, and Midori's only sister had died at a young age, so Suguha had no concept of cousins. When she suddenly learned that Kazuto was the son of her mother's sister, she couldn't immediately grasp the distance of that distinction. Part of her felt he was infinitely more distant, and part of her thought there was no difference at all. She still couldn't put her relationship with Kazuto into words.

But...no. There was *one* thing that had changed...

Suguha swung her sword sharper than before, trying to jolt herself away from that train of thought before it took root. She was afraid of where that would lead her, so she focused her mind on the sensations of her body and kept swinging.

By the time she finished her allotted number of swings, the angle of the morning sun was quite different. She wiped away the sweat on her brow as she put down the *shinai*, and then turned to see...

"Ah..."

Suguha froze the instant she looked back to the house.

At some point, Kazuto had sat down on the edge of the porch, clad in sweats, watching her. When their eyes met, he smiled and said, "Morning."

He tossed her a small bottle of mineral water, and she caught it with her left hand.

"G-good morning. You should have said something if you were watching."

"You looked so serious, I didn't want to disturb you."

"Trust me, it's all automatic to me at this point..."

Suguha was secretly pleased that they'd been able to manage easy conversations like this naturally over the last two months, but she still sat at an awkward distance from him. She set down the *shinai* and twisted the cap off the bottle, feeling the cold water permeate her flushed body as it passed her lips.

"Yeah, I guess so. You've been doing it this entire time…"

Kazuto picked up her *shinai* and gave it a quick swing, still sitting down. He looked instantly perplexed.

"Too light…"

"Huh?" Suguha pulled away from the bottle to stare at him. "That's a true bamboo blade, so it's on the heavy side. The carbon fiber ones are almost two ounces lighter."

"Oh, right. I meant, uh…comparatively speaking."

He suddenly snatched the bottle of water from her hands and downed the rest of it in one mouthful.

"Hey…" She felt her cheeks burn and questioned him in order to hide it. "Compared to what?"

He didn't answer, placing the bottle on the porch and getting to his feet. "Say, you wanna have a go?"

She looked up at him, dumbfounded. "Have a go? Like…a match?"

"Exactly."

Kazuto never had much of an interest in kendo, but he spoke as though the idea were commonplace.

"With all the equipment and everything…?"

"Hmm, I guess we could try holding back at the last moment… but I'd hate to see you get hurt, Sugu. We still have Grandpa's old gear, right? Let's do it in the dojo."

Suguha quickly forgot her confusion and trepidation over his sudden idea, and a grin crossed her lips.

"Are you sure? It's been a while for you, hasn't it? And you want to face one of the national quarterfinalists? Will there be any contest? Besides…" She looked concerned. "Can your body handle it? You shouldn't push yourself…"

"Heh! I gotta show off the results of all that muscle-building rehab."

He smirked and began trotting off to the building around the back of the house. Suguha hurried after him.

The Kirigaya family plot was larger than it had any right to be,

and to the east of the main house was a small but cozy dojo. Their grandfather's will had made it absolutely clear that the building was not to be torn down, so Suguha used it for her everyday practice, and it was therefore well maintained.

They stepped into the dojo barefooted, performed the customary bow, and started preparing for their duel. Fortunately, their late grandfather had been about Kazuto's size, so he found a set of armor that, while dusty, was a good fit for him. They finished tightening the strings on their helmets at the same time and faced each other in the center of the room. Another bow.

Suguha rose from the formal kneeling position and held her beloved *shinai* at mid-level. Kazuto, meanwhile…

"What's that supposed to be, big brother?"

The moment Suguha saw Kazuto's stance, she burst out chuckling. It was absolutely bizarre. His left foot was extended forward, his right foot back. His waist was crouched, the tip of the *shinai* in his right hand nearly touching the floorboards, while his left hand was merely placed on the hilt.

"If there were a judge here, he'd totally chew you out!"

"Good thing there isn't. This is my own personal style."

Suguha resumed her position in disbelief. Kazuto spread his feet even farther, lowering his center of gravity.

Just as she steeled her back foot for a forward pounce that would easily catch his helpless helmet, Suguha hesitated. Kazuto's stance was preposterous, but there was a kind of ease about it. His defense appeared full of easily exploitable holes, but she felt she couldn't just charge forward without caution. It was as though he was utilizing a stance he'd practiced for years and years…

But that couldn't be right. Kazuto had only practiced kendo for two years, from age seven to eight. He wouldn't have learned anything but the very basics.

He suddenly sprang into motion, as though sensing her hesitation. Kazuto slid forward, still low, his *shinai* springing upward from the right. His speed itself wasn't surprising, but the motion was, and Suguha was caught flat-footed. She could only act on reflex.

"Teya!!"

From her open right foot, she swung down at Kazuto's left gauntlet. Her timing was perfect—or it would have been if she hadn't hit empty air.

His dodge was impossible. Kazuto pulled his left hand off the hilt of the *shinai* and pulled it in close to his body. That shouldn't be possible. Now his *shinai* shot forward at Suguha's exposed helmet. She craned her neck hastily to avoid it.

They circled around and pulled back to allow a space between them. Suguha's mind had switched to a different mode altogether. There was a pleasant, familiar tension present, all the blood in her body threatening to boil. This time it was her turn to attack. She unleashed her best, a "kote men" strike from gauntlet to helmet—

But Kazuto evaded it cleanly once again. He pulled back his arm, twisted his body, and avoided the point of her blade by the width of a hair. Secretly, Suguha was shocked. She was known on her team for the quickness of her strikes, and she couldn't remember the last time she'd missed on multiple attacks in such a spectacular manner.

Now she struck powerfully, in full attack mode. The tip of her sword flashed at breathless speed. But Kazuto dodged each and every strike. Glancing at his eyes through the helmet's mask, Suguha thought that he saw every one with perfect precision.

Irritated, she came in close to catch hilt on hilt. The pressure of Suguha's powerful legs and core pushed Kazuto off-balance. Without missing a beat, she unleashed a powerful overhead blow.

"Yaaah!!"

By the time she came to her senses, it was too late. The uncompromising swing caught Kazuto flush on the center of his mask. A high-pitched *thwack* echoed through the dojo.

He stumbled backward several steps until he managed to regain his balance.

"Oh my gosh, are you okay?" she cried, but he waved a hand in easy reassurance.

"Wow...I give. You're really tough, Sugu. Heathcliff's got nothing on you."

"Are you sure you're all right...?"

"Yeah. Let's call it a day, though."

Kazuto took several steps backward and did something even more bizarre. He whipped the *shinai* back and forth, then attempted to place it over his back. The next moment, he froze, then scratched the outside of his helmet. Now Suguha was really worried.

"Are you sure that blow to your head didn't...?"

"N-no, no! It's an old habit." He slumped down to his knees and began untying his guards.

They left the dojo together and headed for the wash station outside the house, splashing water onto their faces to rinse away the sweat. The duel's transition from good fun to deadly serious had left them both feeling plenty warm.

"You really caught me by surprise back there. When did you get to practice like that?"

"Well, my step is good, but the attack still isn't up to snuff. It's a lot harder to re-create those sword skills without system assistance," he muttered cryptically. "Still, that was a lot of fun. Maybe I should pick up kendo again."

"Really? Really, really?!"

Suguha hadn't meant for it to sound that excited. She could tell her face had lost its composure.

"Can you teach me, Sugu?"

"O-of course! Let's do kendo again!"

"Once I put more muscle back on."

Kazuto ruffled her hair, and she grinned. Just the thought of them having practice together again nearly brought her to tears with joy.

"Um, hey, big brother, guess what?"

Suguha didn't know why he had suddenly decided to pick up kendo again, but in her excitement, she was about to reveal her new hobby to him. But abruptly thought better of it and clammed up.

"What?"

"Um, never mind. It's still a secret!"

"Whatever, weirdo."

They walked in the back door of the house, drying their heads off with large towels. Their mother, Midori, always slept until noon-ish, so breakfast was usually Suguha's job, though Kazuto helped alternate now.

"I'm gonna hop in the shower. What're you up to today?"

"Oh... I'm going to... the hospital..."

"..."

She'd asked the question without thinking, and now Suguha's buoyant spirits returned to earth a bit.

"Ah, right. You're going to see her."

"Yep... It's the only thing I *can* do..."

It was about a month ago that Kazuto had told her he'd found his beloved in that other world. They'd been sitting against the wall, side by side, in his room, holding coffee mugs as he told the story in bits and pieces. In the past, Suguha would never have believed you could fall in love with someone in a virtual world. But now, she felt like she understood. What really struck her was the faint glimpse of tears she saw welling in his eyes as he spoke.

They'd been together until the very final moment, Kazuto said. They were supposed to return to the real world hand in hand. But only he came back. She was still sleeping. No one could explain what had happened to her—what was still happening to her. He had visited her in the hospital for three straight days.

Suguha tried to imagine Kazuto sitting at the bedside of his lover, holding her hand, silently calling her name, as she had done to him. Every time she did, she was struck with an indescribable emotion; it was a sharp twinge, striking deep in her heart. Her breathing grew painful. It made her want to hold herself and fall to the floor.

She wanted Kazuto to have a smile on his face forever. He was so changed after his return, so much brighter, that he might as well have been a different person. He talked to Suguha easily, he was shockingly kind, and he didn't seem to be forcing himself to do it.

It was as though they were back to their childhood ways. That was why seeing tears in his eyes was so painful to her, she told herself.

But I already know…

Suguha knew that when he hid his eyes while talking about Her, the pain that welled in her chest came from another, secret emotion.

She silently called out to him as she watched him drinking his cup of milk in the kitchen.

Big brother, I know the truth.

Suguha still wasn't sure what had changed when he went from brother to cousin.

But she did know one thing: something she'd never considered before, but which now perpetually twinkled inside of her secretly.

It was the fact that maybe, just maybe, she was allowed to fall in love with her brother.

———

I took a quick shower, changed, and left the house on the mountain bike I'd bought a month ago. I pedaled slowly and easily to the south. It was a nine-mile trip to my destination, which was a long way to ride on a bike, but it made for good muscle-building rehabilitation.

I was heading for the city of Tokorozawa in Saitama Prefecture— a state-of-the-art general hospital on the outskirts of town. In a room on the top floor, she was quietly sleeping.

Two months earlier, I'd ended the game of death that was Sword Art Online by defeating its final boss, Heathcliff the Paladin, on the seventy-fifth floor of the floating castle Aincrad. Just after that, I awoke in an unfamiliar hospital room and realized that I'd returned to reality.

But she—my game partner, the woman I loved more than any other, Asuna the Flash—did not come with me.

It didn't take long to look up her actual location. After waking in that Tokyo hospital room, I wandered the halls on uncertain legs until the nurses spotted me. In less than an hour, a man in a suit rushed in to see me. He claimed to be from the Ministry of Internal Affairs, SAO Incident Office.

That imposing-sounding organization had been formed soon after the SAO Incident began, but in those two years, they'd been able to accomplish very little. I couldn't blame them. One wrong move attempting to interfere with the server and undo the mastermind Akihiko Kayaba's programmed protection, and ten thousand minds could have been boiled in an instant. No one man could shoulder the responsibility to make that choice.

What they *could* do, however, was arrange for the victims to be taken to adequate hospitals—in itself a remarkable accomplishment of coordination—and monitor what little player data was available to the outside world.

Somehow, they knew my level, my coordinates, and even that I was high up among the "clearers" who were responsible for advancing progress in the game. Which was apparently why, when players held captive suddenly began waking up one day last November, they rushed to my hospital room to ask me what had happened.

I'd given the man in the black-rimmed glasses my conditions. I would tell him everything I knew. In return, he would tell me what I wanted to know.

What I wanted was Asuna's location, naturally. After a few minutes of frantic phone calls, the man came back, clearly unnerved.

"Asuna Yuuki is being held at a medical facility in Tokorozawa. But she hasn't awakened like the others…In fact, there are still three hundred victims around the country who haven't come back yet."

At the very beginning, simple server lag was the hypothesis, given the enormity of the process that had transpired within the game. But as the hours and days went on, no update came on the condition of Asuna and the three hundred like her.

The public was electrified, speculating that Akihiko Kayaba's plot still continued. But I couldn't agree. I'd been there in that world of endless sunset as Aincrad collapsed behind us. I'd talked to him for a few brief minutes, and I recalled the lucidity in his gaze.

Kayaba said that he would release all of the surviving players. At that late hour, he had no reason to lie about it. I took him at his word—that he was prepared to move on from that world and wipe everything clean.

But whether through an unforeseen accident or someone else's design, the main SAO server was not reformatted entirely. It was still an impenetrable black box, working away. In the same way, Asuna's NerveGear still held her spirit prisoner, attached to that server. There was no way for me to know what was going on in there. If only, one more time, I could return to that world...

Suguha would be furious if she knew, but one time I left a note, went into my room, and put my NerveGear back on. I tried loading up the Sword Art Online client, but before my eyes appeared only a simple error message: UNABLE TO CONNECT TO SERVER.

So, as soon as my physical rehab was finished and I was able to get around again, I started visiting Asuna's hospital room as regularly as I could.

The time I spent with her was always painful. Knowing that someone so important to me was spirited away by something cruel and unfeeling left my soul wounded. I could feel it oozing blood. But there was nothing else I could do. As I am now, powerless and minuscule, I was helpless.

After forty minutes of slow, measured pedaling, I turned off the major thoroughfare and onto a smaller road, which wound its way up some hills until a massive building came into view. It was a high-tech medical facility, operated by a private corporation.

I waved at the now-familiar security guard as I passed through the front gate, then parked my bicycle in a corner of the large lot. I got my guest pass from the luxurious first-floor lobby that looked more hotel than hospital and clipped it to my shirt pocket as I strode into the elevator.

The doors opened smoothly, just a few seconds later, on the eighteenth, and highest, floor. An empty hallway continued south. This floor was largely reserved for long-term patients, so it was rare to pass anyone in the halls. Eventually, I reached the end, and a pale green door came into view. There was a dully glowing nameplate on the wall next to the door.

Yuuki, Asuna. Beneath the name, a single slot. I took the pass off my chest and slid it through the reader. A chime sounded, and the door automatically retracted.

One step inside and I was surrounded by the cool scent of flowers. Despite the midwinter season, the room was positively exploding with real, fresh flowers. Farther inside the spacious room, a curtain was drawn, and I approached it slowly.

Please let her be awake in there. I put my hand on the curtain, praying for a miracle. Silently, it parted.

It was a state-of-the-art bed designed for full patient care. The surface was a gel material, the same as mine had been. A clean white comforter was glowing softly in the sunlight. She was underneath it, sleeping.

The first time I'd visited this place, I was struck by the sudden thought that she might not want me to see her real-life body while she was unconscious. But that concern was completely banished from my mind when I saw how beautiful she looked.

Her rich, lustrous chestnut hair was splayed softly across the support cushions. Her skin was so pale, you could nearly see through it, but the hospital's gentle care kept it from having a sickly tinge. There was even a hint of rose color in her cheeks.

She didn't seem to have lost as much weight as I had. The slender line from her neck to collarbone was just as I remembered it in the virtual world. Light pink lips. Long eyelashes. It almost seemed like they might tremble and pop open at any moment—if not for the navy blue headgear that covered her skull.

All three indicator lights on the NerveGear were shining blue. The occasional starlike twinkle was proof that the connection was functioning. Even now, her soul was held captive in another world.

I took her fragile hand in both of mine. There was a slight warmth to it. It was no different from the hand I remembered— the one that clung to mine, that touched my body, that slipped around my back. My breath caught, and I desperately held back the tears.

"Asuna…"

The faint alarm of the bedside clock brought me back to my senses. My eyes snapped to it and I was surprised to find it was already noon.

"I've got to go now, Asuna. I'll be back soon…"

As I stood to leave, the door opened behind me. I turned around to see two men entering the room.

"Ahh, you're here, Kirigaya. As always, I appreciate your concern."

A smile split the face of the solid middle-aged man in front. He wore a well-tailored three-piece brown suit, and the tightness of his face despite his stocky build suggested the vitality of a very successful man. Only the silver in his slicked-back hair revealed the mental toll that the last two years had taken.

He was Shouzou Yuuki, Asuna's father. She had mentioned once or twice that he was an entrepreneur, but even then, I couldn't hide my shock when I learned that he was actually the CEO of the electronics manufacturer RCT.

I gave him a polite bow and said, "Good afternoon. Sorry to have disturbed you, Mr. Yuuki."

"Not at all. Come any time you like. I'm sure she's happy."

He approached Asuna's bedside and tenderly stroked her hair. All was quiet for a moment, then he looked up and motioned to the other man with him.

"You haven't met, have you? This is Sugou, the manager of our lab."

My first impression was that he seemed quite nice. He was tall, clad in a dark gray suit, with frameless glasses resting on his long face. The eyes behind the thin lenses were narrow lines, which made it seem as though he were smiling all the time. He was quite young—not yet thirty, by my estimation.

Sugou extended a hand to me and said, "Nice to meet you. I'm Nobuyuki Sugou. So you're *the* hero, Kirito."

"...Kazuto Kirigaya. Nice to meet you."

I glanced at Shouzou as I shook Sugou's hand. He inclined his head slightly as he stroked his chin.

"Oops, sorry 'bout that. I know, stuff that happened in the SAO servers is all confidential. But it was such a dramatic tale that it's hard not to talk about it. He's the son of a very good friend of mine. Our families have been close for years."

"About that, sir." Sugou turned to Shouzou, releasing my hand. "I was hoping we could get everything official by the end of next month."

"I see...and you're sure about this? You're still so young; there's plenty of time to start a new life."

"My heart has been set on this for years. I'd like to be able to put Asuna in that dress...while she's still so beautiful."

"...Indeed. It might be time to make a hard decision."

I listened to their conversation, unsure of what they were discussing. Shouzou looked back to me.

"Well, it's time I ought to be going. I'll see you again later, Kirigaya."

With a brisk nod, Shouzou Yuuki turned his imposing bulk around and walked to the door. It opened and shut again. Only the man named Sugou was left.

He slowly paced around the foot of the bed to stand on the other side, then picked up a lock of her hair and started rubbing it audibly with his fingers. Something about the gesture filled me with revulsion.

"I hear you lived together with Asuna inside the game," he said softly, still looking at her.

"...Yes."

"That makes things...complicated...between us, then."

He raised his head and stared into my eyes. In that instant, I understood that my first impression of this man could not have been more wrong.

Those narrow eyes featured beady pupils that gave him a wicked glare. Both corners of his mouth curled upward into a grin that could not be described with any word other than *devious*. A chill ran up my spine.

"You see, the matter I mentioned a moment ago . . ." He gloated. "It regards my marriage to Asuna."

I was struck speechless. What in the world was he talking about? The meaning of his words only slowly penetrated my skin, like freezing air. After several seconds of silence, I haltingly found my voice.

"You can't . . . possibly . . ."

"True. Legally, we cannot be married because Asuna is not conscious and cannot give consent. On paper, the Yuuki family is simply taking me in as a foster son. As a matter of fact, she's always hated me."

He traced a finger along Asuna's cheek.

"Her parents never seemed to have a clue. But I always knew that if the topic of marriage came up, there was a high likelihood she'd reject it. Which is exactly why this situation suits my ends so well. I hope she sleeps for a while yet."

His finger got closer and closer to her lips.

"Stop it!"

I grabbed his hand without thinking and pulled it away from her face. My voice was hoarse with anger.

"Are you saying . . . you're taking *advantage* of Asuna's coma?"

Sugou leered again as he snatched his hand away. "Advantage? Actually, it's entirely within my legal right. Kirigaya, are you aware of what happened to Argus, the developers of SAO?"

"I heard they were dissolved."

"Yes. In addition to the development costs, the astronomical reparations for the Incident drove them bankrupt. Maintaining the SAO server was consigned to RCT's full-dive engineering team: my department."

Sugou circled around the headboard of the bed to face me. He stuck his face up close to mine, still wearing that demonic smirk.

"Meaning that Asuna's life is now entirely under my supervision and control. And doesn't that entitle me to just the tiniest amount of compensation?" he whispered into my ear, and I knew.

He was using Asuna's helpless predicament, her very life, for his own selfish ends.

As I stood, petrified in shock, Sugou finally shed the leer he'd been wearing and spoke icily.

"I have no idea what kind of promises you two made while you were inside the game, but I'd appreciate it if you stopped visiting the hospital. And please keep your distance from the Yuuki family."

I clenched my fists, but there was nothing I could do. Several glacial seconds passed. Eventually, Sugou pulled away, his cheek dimpling as though he were about to burst into laughter.

"We'll have the ceremony here at the hospital next month. Tell you what: I'll shoot you an invitation. I've got to be off, so get the most out of your final meeting—*hero*."

I wish I had my swords, I thought desperately. *I'd run him through the heart with one and cut off his head with the other.* Cognizant of my rage or not, Sugou patted me on the shoulder and left the room.

I had no memory of the trip home. The next thing I knew, I was sitting on my bed, staring at the wall.

My marriage to Asuna.

Asuna's life is now entirely under my supervision and control.

His words echoed through my head, over and over. Each time they did, I was pierced with hatred as sharp and hot as molten metal.

But…maybe my ego was getting the best of me.

Sugou had been close to the Yuuki family for years and was essentially Asuna's fiancé. He had earned Shouzou Yuuki's trust and was in a position of great responsibility at RCT. It had been decided years ago that he would one day marry Asuna, and I was just some kid who she met in an online game. Perhaps the rage I felt, the indignation at losing Asuna, was nothing more than the frustration of a child who had been deprived of his toys.

To us, the floating castle Aincrad was the only world that existed. That's what we believed. The words we traded, the promises we made, all those memories were like shining jewels in my mind.

But the harsh whetstone of reality was grinding them down to size. It chipped away at those jewels.

I want to be with you forever, Kirito, she had said with a smile— a smile that was slowly but surely fading away.

"I'm sorry... I'm so sorry, Asuna. I... can't do anything..."

This time, the tears that I'd been struggling to hold back finally fell, dripping onto my clenched fists.

——※——

"The bath's open, big brother," Suguha called out to the door of Kazuto's second-floor bedroom. There was no answer.

He'd returned from the hospital in the evening but immediately shut himself in his room, and he did not emerge for dinner.

Suguha put her hand on the doorknob, then hesitated. But she told herself that if he was napping untended, he might catch a cold, and so she pushed the knob.

It swiveled and clicked, and the door inched open. It was black inside. She thought he must be sleeping, until a wave of frigid air trickled over her, and she shivered. Kazuto must have left the window open.

Suguha snuck into the room, shaking her head. She closed the door and approached the window on the south side of the room, and she was startled to discover that Kazuto was not lying down asleep but was sitting on the edge of his bed, head slumped.

"Oh, um... sorry, I thought you were sleeping."

After a few moments, Kazuto spoke, his voice ragged and weak.

"Can I just... be alone for a while?"

"B-but it's so cold in here..." Suguha reached out and touched his arm. It was cold as ice. "Oh my gosh, you're freezing! You'll catch a chill. Come on, you need a bath."

It was then that Suguha noticed the nighttime lights coming through the window, shining on Kazuto's cheeks.

"Wh... what's wrong?"

"Nothing," he muttered damply.

"But…"

Kazuto suddenly put his hands to his forehead, as if to block her uncomprehending stare. When he spoke again, it was hard and derisive.

"I'm hopeless… I swore to myself that I wouldn't complain in front of you."

In that instant, Suguha instinctively knew. Softly and hesitantly, she spoke.

"Did something happen… with Asuna?"

His body stiffened. It sounded like he wrung the voice out of his throat.

"Asuna… is going… far away. Far beyond… my grasp…"

That didn't tell her anything specific. But the sight of him curled over, shedding tears like a child, shook Suguha deeply.

She closed the window, drew the curtains, and turned on the heater before sitting next to him on the bed. After a moment's hesitation, she put her arms around his chilly body. She could feel the tension drain out of him.

Suguha whispered into his ear. "C'mon, hang in there. Don't just give up on the one you truly love…"

It took all of her being to find those words, and when they left her mouth and echoed in her ears, the pain threatened to rip her apart. It was the pain of something coming to life within her breast. Suguha was keenly aware of how much she truly loved him at that moment.

I can't keep lying to myself.

She leaned back and softly rolled Kazuto onto the bed, then pulled the covers up. Under their warmth, she put her arm around his back again.

As she gently rubbed his back, his racking sobs transitioned to the peaceful breath of sleep. She closed her eyes and told herself, *I have to give up. I need to bury this deep, deep within me.*

Kazuto's heart belongs to her, not me.

A single tear of her own dripped down Suguha's cheek and landed on the sheets.

—◦◦◦—

I drifted through a sweet and pleasant warmth.

It was the wonderful sensation of floating just before waking up. The sunlight trickling through the forest branches gently caressed my cheek.

I leaned closer to embrace her as she slept next to me. Her breath was steady with sleep, and I opened my eyes to see…

"Wha—?"

I caught the yelp in my throat and leaped back a foot or two, still on my back. The next second, I sprung up to a sitting position and looked around wildly.

It wasn't the same old forest on the twenty-second floor of Aincrad I always dreamed about. I was in my actual room, in my actual bed…but I wasn't alone.

I carefully lifted the blanket, still shocked, but I put it back down just as quickly, so that I could shake my head to clear the cobwebs of sleep. I pulled the cover back again: short black hair. Vivid eyebrows.

Suguha was fast asleep, wearing her pajamas, face buried in my pillow.

"Wh-what the *hell*'s going on here…?"

I desperately tried to remember what had happened last night. Right—I seemed to remember having a conversation with Suguha after coming home from the hospital. I'd been lost in angst, and Suguha had done her best to console me. After that, I must have fallen asleep…

"What am I, a little kid…?"

After a brief bout of utter mortification, I looked back at Suguha's innocent, sleeping face. Surely she didn't need to sleep in the same bed to comfort me…

Thinking back, a similar thing had happened to me in Aincrad. There was the beast-tamer I met around the fortieth floor. She'd reminded me of Suguha. She'd also fallen asleep in my bed, and I had been just as confused about what to do then.

I couldn't help but smile. Asuna and Sugou were still weighing heavily on my mind, but the chest-rending ache had somehow melted away overnight.

All the memories of what had happened in Aincrad were like precious jewels to me, whether happy or sad. The important thing was that they were all true memories. I couldn't disparage them myself. I swore to Asuna that we would meet again in the real world. There must still be something I could do about this.

Suddenly, Suguha's last words before I fell asleep echoed in my ears.

Don't just give up…

"Yeah…you're right," I muttered, leaning forward to poke Suguha's cheek. "Get up, Sugu, it's morning."

"Nng," she grunted unhappily, trying to pull the blanket over her head. This time, I pinched her cheek and pulled it.

"Wake up. You're wasting valuable morning practice time."

"Muhh…"

Suguha finally open a bleary eye.

"Oh…good morning, big brother," she murmured, sitting upright.

She peered at me quizzically for a moment, then began looking around the room. Eventually, her tired eyes bulged wide. Her cheeks grew redder and redder.

"Ah—! Um—! I didn't—!"

Suguha was red to the ears, her mouth working soundlessly. She finally leaped to her feet and exploded out of the room with a massive crash.

"Sheesh." I scratched my head, getting to my feet. I opened my window and took a deep breath, letting the cold air flow over my lethargic limbs.

I was laying out a fresh outfit to change into after an impending quick shower when I received The Notice.

An electronic *ding* sounded behind me, and I turned to my desk. The e-mail indicator on the upper frame of my panel PC was blinking. I sat down in the chair and brushed the mouse to activate the monitor.

Computers had changed quite a bit in the two years I'd been "away." The final nail had been driven into the coffin of classic hard-drive storage, and even its successor, the solid-state drive, had been phased out for high-speed MRAM. This meant that there was no longer any discernible lag time of any kind while computing. The instant I activated the mail program, my inbox was fully refreshed, descending in chronological order. The sender of the latest message at the bottom of the screen was someone familiar: Agil.

Agil the ax warrior had run a general store in Algade, the main town of the fiftieth floor of Aincrad. I'd met up with him in Tokyo about three weeks earlier. We'd traded e-mail contacts at the time, but this was the first message I'd actually received from him. It was titled, "Look at this." Perhaps he'd been in a hurry when he sent it, because there wasn't a single word in the body of the message, only a picture attachment.

Curious, I opened the picture in the viewer. The next instant, I rose from the chair and craned closer to the screen to get a better look.

It was a mysterious image. The bold coloring and lighting told me it was not a photograph but a screenshot of a virtual, polygonal world. In the foreground were blurry, unfocused golden bars. Behind them was a white table and chair. Sitting in the chair was a woman wearing a dress in the same shade of white. But the glimpse of her side profile through the bars looked just like—

"Asuna…?"

The resolution was rough; it seemed to be a section of a much larger picture zoomed in considerably. But I would recognize that long chestnut hair anywhere. Her hands were folded on top of the table, and her face looked lost in grief. Upon closer examination, she seemed to have translucent wings sprouting from her back.

I grabbed my portable terminal off the desk and scrolled through my phone listings impatiently. The few seconds of dial tone seemed interminable. After a click, I heard Agil's deep voice.

"Hel—"

"What is this picture?!"

"...Normally it's good manners to say who's calling first, Kirito."

"No time! Just tell me!"

"Look, it's a long story. Can you come to my place?"

"I'll be there. I'm leaving now."

I hung up without waiting for a response and picked up my clothes. After the world's fastest shower, I slipped on my shoes and hopped onto my bike, hair still dripping. The familiar route to the train station had never felt so long.

Agil's café-and-bar was located in a crowded alley in the neighborhood of Okachi, in the Taito ward of Tokyo. The storefront was made of sooty black wood, and only a small metallic sign affixed over the doorway indicated that there was a business there at all. The sign was decorated in the shape of two dice, reading DICEY CAFÉ.

A dry chime sounded when I pushed open the door. The large bald man behind the counter looked up and grinned at my entrance. There was no one else inside.

"Hey, that was quick."

"This place is as empty as the last time I visited. I'm amazed it stayed open for the last two years."

"Shut up, we do a brisk night business."

Our lighthearted ribbing was just as it had been in the other world.

I'd tried reaching out to Agil late the previous month. An agent from the Ministry of Internal Affairs had succeeded in getting me a list of the names and addresses of as many in-game friends as I could remember. No doubt plenty of players were seeking to reunite with Klein, Nishida, Silica, and Lisbeth, but I'd decided to give them more time to get back to regular life before contacting them. When I'd brought up the topic on my first visit, Agil had retorted, "Oh, so I don't merit that kind of consideration?"

When I learned that Agil—real name Andrew Gilbert Mills—also ran a business in real life, it made perfect sense. He was pure

African-American but also a second-generation native of Tokyo, and he'd opened his combination café-and-bar in the familiar neighborhood of Okachi when he was twenty-five. He had been blessed with a steady clientele and a beautiful wife, and just when everything seemed poised to take off, he fell prisoner to Sword Art Online. When he finally returned after those two years in the game, he'd expected the business to be gone, but his wife had rolled up her sleeves and kept the store running the entire time. The story warmed my heart.

It was the type of place with plenty of regulars. The wood fixtures had the deep luster of polish and care, and the cozy intimacy of the interior, with only four tables and a counter, made it a comfortable visit.

I pulled up a leather-seated stool, impatiently called for a coffee, and launched into the topic at hand.

"What did that mean?"

He didn't answer. Instead, he reached under the counter and pulled out a rectangular package that he slid over to me. I stopped it with a finger.

The package fit in the palm of my hand, clearly a video-game box. I scanned it for a platform and noticed a logo in the upper right corner that said AMUSPHERE.

"Never heard of this console..."

"That's because the AmuSphere was released while we were on the other side. It's a successor to the NerveGear."

"..."

Agil gave me a quick explanation as I eyed with suspicion the logo of two interlocking rings.

After the disaster it had caused, the NerveGear was vilified far and wide, a demonic machine of enslavement. But apparently the market had spoken, and there was still a demand for full-dive VR gaming. Barely half a year into the SAO Incident, a different hardware company unveiled its own model, "but safe this time," to such resounding success that traditional TV consoles were now a minority share of the game industry. This AmuSphere was a major force in gaming, thanks in part to many titles in the same genre as SAO.

It all made sense to me, but I was in no rush to learn more. I didn't ever want to relive that particular experience.

"So this is another VRMMO, then?"

I took another look at the case. The front cover was an illustration of a large full moon rising above a deep, deep forest. A boy and girl holding swords were caught in silhouette, flying across the golden disk. They were dressed in typical fantasy garb, and large, translucent wings sprang from their backs. An ornate logo adorned the bottom of the cover: ALFHEIM ONLINE.

"ALf...heim...Online? What does it mean?"

"It's actually pronounced more like *Alv-heym*. Means 'land of the fairies,' apparently."

"Fairies, huh...? Sounds pretty laid-back. One of those casual MMOs?"

"Believe it or not, just the opposite. It's actually pretty hard-core."

Agil placed a steaming cup in front of me and grinned. I lifted it up and breathed in the scent before inquiring further.

"What makes it hard-core?"

"Totally skill-based. Player skill is rewarded, PK-ing is encouraged."

"Meaning...?"

"You don't have a 'level.' You can only power up skills through use, and your HP barely increases as you play through the game. Battle depends on the player's actual athletic ability. It's like SAO with magic and no sword skills. People say the graphics and animation are almost on par with SAO, too."

"Wow...sounds impressive."

I puckered my lips into a soundless whistle. The floating castle Aincrad was the creation of the genius Akihiko Kayaba's fanatic obsession. It was hard to imagine that another developer could create a VR world with the same fidelity.

"How is PK-ing encouraged?"

"When you create your character, you choose from a number of fairy species, and you're allowed to kill the other kinds."

"Wow, that does sound hard-core. But a game like that won't sell big, even with great production values. Not if it's designed for such a niche market," I opined critically, but Agil's wide mouth grinned again.

"That's what I thought, too, but it's been selling like gangbusters. The thing is, you can fly in the game."

"Fly...?"

"Everyone's a fairy, so they have wings. It's got some kind of in-game flight engine, and once you get used to it, you can fly around freely without a controller."

At this, I couldn't help but exclaim in fascination. Plenty of flying games had come to market after the release of the NerveGear, but all of them were flight simulators that involved manipulating a device of some kind. The reason no games offered players the ability to fly directly was simple: Human beings don't have wings.

In a virtual world, players' actions are faithfully translated to mirror their real bodies. But this meant that what was impossible in life was still impossible in the game. The developer might slap some wings onto your model, but what human muscles are supposed to work a pair of wings?

By the end of SAO, Asuna and I had raised our jumping power high enough that we could mimic "flying" in a way, but this was simply an extension of a jump trajectory, not true flight.

"That sounds incredible. How do you control the wings?"

"Dunno, but it's apparently pretty hard. They say new players have to control it with a flight stick in one hand."

"..."

For an instant, I was actually eager for the chance to try it out. I quickly downed a hot swig of coffee to extinguish that fire.

"Okay, so that's the game. But more to the point, what was that picture?"

Agil reached under the counter again and pulled out a sheet of paper that he placed on the bar. It was glossy with printing film. The same picture.

"What do you think?" Agil asked. I stared at it for several moments.

"She looks...like Asuna."

"So you agree. It's a screenshot from the game, so I can't blow it up any larger, unfortunately."

"Just tell me, where was it taken?"

"In there. Inside ALfheim Online."

Agil took the game box from me and flipped it over. In the center of the back cover, surrounded by the game description and screenshots, was an illustration of what appeared to be the game world. The round map was split into territories for each of the fairy races, extending radially outward from a massive tree in the middle.

"They call it the World Tree," Agil said, tapping the image. "The player's goal is to reach the land atop the tree before the other races can get there."

"Don't they just fly?"

"Seems there's a limit on your flight time. You can't fly forever. In fact, you can't even reach the lowest branch of the tree that way. But there's always some idiot who wants to try. I heard about a group of five who stood on one another's shoulders, lightest to heaviest, and tried to reach the branches like a rocket with fuel tanks."

"Ha-ha! I see...That's pretty smart, for being so stupid."

"Well, their plan was good, and they got real close to the branches. They didn't quite reach the lowest one, but the fifth and final person took some screens as proof of the altitude. One of the shots showed something strange: an enormous birdcage hanging from one of the branches."

"A birdcage..."

My eyebrows knitted at the ominous implications of that word. *Trapped in a birdcage.*

"And after the screenshot was zoomed in as far as it could go, that's what was left."

"But this is a legitimate game, right? Why would Asuna be in there?"

I grabbed the box and took another look. I scanned the bottom of the rectangular case. The name of the developer was RCT Progress.

"Kirito, what's with the glare?"

"Nothin'. Got any other pictures, Agil? Anything that might show others like Asuna, who never returned from SAO, held captive within this ALfheim Online game?"

The shopkeeper's heavy brow furrowed as he shook his head. "Haven't heard of anything. But we'd know for sure if I did—you bet your ass I'd have called the police instead of you."

"Yeah...I'm sure you would have..."

But as I nodded, my mind was racing back to Nobuyuki Sugou's words.

The SAO servers are currently under my control, he had said. But "under control" was a misleading description. The server itself was still a black box, impervious to any outside interference, as I understood it.

It suited his ends to have Asuna asleep inside the machine. And now a girl who looks like Asuna was sighted in another VRMMO, run by the publishing arm of RCT...Could it truly just be a coincidence?

For an instant, I thought I might contact the rescue team in the Ministry, until I realized just how little proof I had to show them.

I looked up, into the face of the burly café owner.

"Agil, can I have this game?"

"Be my guest. You going in?"

"Yeah. I need to see it for myself."

Agil briefly looked concerned. I understood how he felt. Part of me felt it was crazy, but there was no denying the tendrils of fear I could sense licking at my feet—there was something going on here.

I shook off the foreboding and gave him a grin.

"A game where death isn't permanent? People these days are spoiled. Guess I'm in the market for a new game console."

"Don't worry, AmuSphere games will run on a NerveGear. It's basically just the same unit with strengthened security."

"Great, that saves me some money," I quipped. This time it was Agil's turn to give me a wry grin.

"If you've got the guts to put on that helmet again, that is."

"I've done it a dozen times already."

That was the truth. I had put on the NerveGear multiple times, just with a net connection, not booted into a game. My vain hope was that Asuna would have sent me a message of some kind. There was nothing, of course. No voice, no text.

But I was done with waiting. I downed the last of my coffee and stood up. The establishment wasn't fancy enough for any kind of electronic money-exchanging systems, so I had to reach into my pocket for some coins to slap on the counter.

"Well, I'm off. Thanks for the coffee—and let me know if you learn anything else."

"I'll put that tip on your tab. Just make sure you rescue Asuna. Otherwise our fight isn't over."

"Yeah...we need to have an offline meet-up here someday."

We bumped fists, and I turned to head out the door.

—◈—

Suguha was lying facedown on her own bed, face buried in her pillow, as she kicked her legs in anguish for minutes at a time.

It was nearly noon, but she was still wearing her pajamas. It was Monday, January 20th, well past the end of winter vacation, but Suguha's middle school made attendance optional just before the end of the school year for graduating students. They were all busy with entrance exams for high school, and if she went to campus, it would only be to pop her head into the kendo club.

She replayed the memory inside her mind for the umpteenth time.

She'd curled up beneath Kazuto's covers with him last night, trying to warm up his freezing body by snuggling close, and then fell asleep. It was the first time she'd ever truly cursed her ability to zonk out ten seconds after lying down.

I'm so stupid, stupid, stupid! she wailed soundlessly, beating her pillow with both hands.

If she'd just woken up before Kazuto, she could have made a silent escape before he noticed. Instead, he had to wake her up and point out that she was in his bed. There was no way she could look at him again.

Embarrassment, shyness, and an undeniable feeling of his sweetness raced around inside of her, gripping her chest so painfully she couldn't breathe. If she folded her arms around her head, she thought she could smell her brother on her pajamas. That only made things worse.

I need to swing my shinai *and clear my head*, she decided, and finally got to her feet. Suguha liked practicing in the dojo because it put her mind in the right state, but she decided the most important thing was to get outside as soon as possible, so she slipped into her tracksuit.

Kazuto was off on some personal business, her mother, Midori, always left for work in the morning, and her father, Minetaka, went back to America after the holidays, so she was alone in the house. She grabbed a cheese muffin from the basket on the dining table downstairs, stuffed it crudely into her mouth, and grabbed a box of orange juice on her way out to the backyard.

Just when she had taken her first big bite, Kazuto walked his bike around the side of the house. Their eyes met.

"Mmfg!"

A piece of muffin caught in her throat, and she coughed. She scrambled to take a swig of orange juice and wash it down, then realized she hadn't popped the straw through the foil on top yet.

"Mmp, mllp!"

"Oh, come on."

Kazuto strode over and snatched the juice box. He stuck one

of the ends of the straw into the lid and the other into Suguha's mouth. She desperately sucked down the cold liquid until she could finally swallow the morsel.

"*Pwah!* I...I thought I was gonna choke to death..."

"Man, you're so clumsy. You don't have to wolf it down all at once."

"Ugh," she muttered. Kazuto sat down next to her and started untying his shoes. She watched him out of the corner of her eye as she took another bite of muffin.

Abruptly, he said, "About last night, Sugu..."

She took another hasty drink of juice before she could start coughing again.

"Y-yes?"

"Well, um...thanks."

"Huh...?"

Suguha was not expecting this. She peered at him curiously.

"Thanks for cheering me up yesterday. It really helped. I'm not going to give up. I'll keep going until I've rescued Asuna."

She smiled to cover up the throb of pain in her chest.

"Good. Keep at it. I've always wanted to meet her."

"I'm sure you'll be great friends." He scrunched her hair and stood up. "Well, see you later."

Suguha turned and watched him go up the stairs, then popped the last bite of muffin into her mouth.

And am I allowed to keep at it, too...?

She headed through the yard to do her stretches at the side of the pond. Once she was nice and warmed up, she picked up the *shinai* and started swinging.

Normally, the steady pattern of thorough swiping would clear her head of all distractions, but this time, the thoughts stayed put.

Am I really allowed to fall in love with him?

She thought she was ready, for a moment, to forget last night—cradling him in bed. Asuna was the only person in Kazuto's heart, a fact of which she was painfully aware.

But...I don't think that matters to me.

She didn't know why Kazuto was weighing so heavily on her mind these days. But her feelings had become as clear as day to her.

When the hospital had called two months ago, Suguha had raced out of the house without waiting for her mother. Kazuto had smiled at her on his hospital bed when he saw her, tears in his eyes. He'd reached out and said, "Sugu," in that familiar voice... and that was when these feelings had been born inside of her. She wanted to be with him always. She wanted to talk with him more. But forcing that on him... She couldn't.

I'm fine just watching him, she told herself as she swung the wooden blade through empty space. She stopped briefly to check the clock in the living room. It was past noon.

"Ah, crap. I forgot my promise," she muttered. She put down the sword and wiped off her sweat with the towel hanging on the pine branch. Up in the sky, the first glimpse of blue was peeking through the clouds.

—◦w◦—

Back in my room, I changed into street clothes, set my phone to away mode, and sat on my bed. I zipped open my backpack and pulled out the game Agil gave me. ALfheim Online.

From what he'd said, it sounded like a pretty serious endeavor. No level system was a big plus for me, though, as it suggested I wouldn't be too inconvenienced by having started it later than everyone else in the game.

Normally with an MMORPG, before starting I'd want to read up on as much information as I could find on the net or in magazines, but I was in no mood for that. I opened the package, pulled out a tiny ROM card, and slid it into a small slot on the Nerve-Gear. After a few seconds, the LED on the front stopped blinking and went solid.

I lay back on the bed and held the device right over my face. It had once been a gleaming navy blue marvel, but now the paint was chipping off here and there. This was the set of shackles that had held me prisoner for two years—but it was also an old friend that had been through hell with me without ever malfunctioning.

Lend me your strength just one more time, I pleaded silently and lowered the NerveGear onto my head. Next came the chin harness, then the visor shield. I shut my eyes.

My heart racing with excitement and unease, I gave the command to begin the game.

"Link start!"

The murky light shining through my closed eyelids abruptly vanished. The signals coming from my optic nerves were canceled, and true darkness enveloped me.

But just as abruptly, a rainbow of color danced before my view. The amorphous light fashioned itself into the NerveGear logo. It was dim and hazy at first but then grew sharper as the device's connection to the visual center of my brain became more solid. Eventually, a small message beneath the logo appeared, signaling that visual connection had been established.

Next came an eerie echoing noise from nowhere in particular. It seemed to be rushing closer, and the warped sound changed pitch until it formed a pleasing harmony. The solemn start-up jingle played and abruptly finished. Audio connection established.

Now the setup moved on to physical sensation, then gravity. The feeling of the bed on my back and the weight of my body disappeared. As each one of my senses was calibrated and tested, the check marks piled up. In time, full-dive tech would no doubt shorten this process considerably, but at this point there was nothing I could do but wait for the headgear to perform its little handshake with each section of my brain in turn.

When the final OK message appeared at last, I was plunged down into darkness. Eventually, a glowing circle of rainbow light appeared from below, and after passing through it, my virtual feet landed in a different world.

Technically, it was just a stage for account creation, still shrouded in darkness. The ALfheim Online logo hung overhead, and a gentle female voice welcomed me to the game.

I followed the computerized voice's instructions and initiated the account and character creation process. A pale blue holo-keyboard materialized at chest height and asked me to input a user ID and password. I typed in the familiar string of letters that I'd used at the start of SAO. If this were an all-digital MMO, I'd be greeted with payment options at this point, but the retail version of ALO came with a free month of play.

Next came my character name. I started to type "Kirito" but hesitated. Very few people knew that Kazuto Kirigaya in the real world went by Kirito online. Only the rescue team from the Ministry of Internal Affairs; Shouzou Yuuki, the president of RCT, who had been closely involved with that team; and Sugou. After that, it was Agil and the still-sleeping Asuna. Even Suguha and my parents didn't know.

Nothing about what had happened in SAO had been made public, especially not character names. There had been countless battles between characters within the game, battles that led to a shocking number of actual deaths in the real world. If stories of who had murdered whom became public, it would no doubt set off a tangle of endless court cases.

For the moment, all charges of murder related to the SAO Incident were laid solely at the feet of the still-missing Akihiko Kayaba. All damages claimed by the families of the victims were levied from Argus, the developer of the game, and it wasn't long until Argus had gone bankrupt. Kayaba had built up Argus into one of the premier development houses and then leveled it to the ground. But as far as the government was concerned, they didn't want the ugly possibility of players suing one another.

I was concerned about Nobuyuki Sugou finding me, but the name itself wasn't that remarkable, so I decided to go ahead and call myself "Kirito." I chose male for my gender, of course.

Next, the female voice instructed me to create my character. Yet, my only choice was player race. All of my cosmetic parameters would be chosen at random, and if I didn't like what I was given, I'd have to pay an in-game fee to re-create the looks I wanted. In this case, I didn't particularly care what I looked like.

I had a choice of nine different fairy-themed races for my character. Each one had its own advantages and disadvantages, the voice said. Some of the names, like salamander, sylph, and gnome, were familiar RPG terms, while others—cait sith, leprechaun—were less so.

The choice didn't matter to me, as I had no intention of playing the game seriously. But I liked the all-black motif of the spriggan starting equipment, so I chose that one and hit OK.

With all the customization complete, the computerized voice wished me luck, and another vortex of light surrounded me. According to the explanation, each race was teleported to its own starting city. The sensation of ground beneath my feet vanished, and I was weightless for a moment before gravity pulled me down. A new world began to take shape from the light. I was in the air, over a small town shrouded in darkness.

I could feel my first sensations of full-dive gameplay in two months sharpening every virtual nerve that had once been so honed by my last experience. The narrow steeples of the castle at the center of town grew closer.

When, suddenly—

The image froze solid. Tiny shards of polygonal material splintered away, and digital noise crawled over my vision like lightning. The level of detail in the game grew cruder and cruder until it resembled a digital mosaic. The world melted and crumbled away.

"Wh-what is this?" I wailed and abruptly felt myself plunging again. I fell down and down, endless blackness beneath me.

"What the hell's going on heeere—"

My helpless scream was swallowed by the void and snuffed into silence.

2

The massive moon hanging in the sky painted the deep forest blue, like the seafloor.

Nights in Alfheim were short, but it would be a while yet until dawn brought its light. The darkness of the forest was normally an eerie thing, but on the run, its concealment was a blessing.

Leafa looked into the starry sky from the shadows of an especially large tree. She couldn't see any foreboding shapes crossing the sky for now. She whispered to her party companion as quietly as she could.

"Get ready. We're going to fly as soon as our wings are recharged."

"B-but I'm still dizzy...," he whined.

"Are you still feeling sick? Oh, this is just sad... When are you going to get used to it, Recon?"

"I can't help it if I'm afraid of flying..."

Leafa sighed in exasperation.

The boy named Recon, slumped at the foot of the tree, was a real-life friend of Leafa's, and they'd started playing ALO—ALfheim Online—at the same time. Meaning that he'd had a year of experience with the game, just like her, and yet he still hadn't conquered his flight sickness. In a game where midair battle skill was everything, his inability to handle more than one or two skirmishes at a time made him largely useless.

But Leafa didn't really mind that part of Recon. If anything, she thought of him like a helpless little brother. His appearance fit his personality perfectly: a short, fragile body, yellow-green hair in a pageboy cut, long drooping ears, and a face that always seemed to be on the verge of tears. For a randomly generated character, his look was so similar to the real thing that the first time she saw him in-game, Leafa nearly laughed her head off.

Then again, according to Recon, Leafa's appearance was fitting as well. She was on the larger side for a sylph, with distinctive eyes and brows.

She'd been hoping for a virtual body that might be described as "willowy," but by all accounts, it was still an attractive character. That was a blessing that required considerable good fortune in this game—many players had sunk several years' worth of monthly fees just on the character reroll cost until they got the look they wanted. So Leafa wasn't about to complain.

Incidentally, avatar appearance had no bearing on performance in ALO, so Recon's battles with dizziness were entirely an issue of his sense of balance.

Leafa reached out and grabbed the back of Recon's chest armor, hauling him to his feet. His four wings were glimmering with pale green light, the game's indication that his flight power had recovered.

"Okay, you're good to go. Our next flight is taking us out of the forest."

"Aww, we must have lost them already. Let's take a break."

"No! One of those salamanders had a really high Search skill, so they might have already found us while we were resting here. We can't handle one more air raid just by ourselves. We need to rush back to our territory!"

"Oh, fine." Recon pouted. He grasped at the air, and a translucent joystick appeared in his hand. It was ALO's flight assistance controller, a short rod with a small ball on the end. He pulled the stick lightly toward himself, and the two pairs of wings on his back fluttered and glowed faintly.

Leafa beat her own wings a few times. Unlike Recon, she didn't need the controller. She had already mastered the art of flying at will, the mark of a first-rate warrior in ALO.

"Let's go!" she commanded, springing into the air. The wings on her back spread to their full width, pushing her upward through the branches toward that full moon. The wind whipped at her cheeks and fluttered her long ponytail.

In a few seconds, she was out in the open, flying above the forest. The land of Alfheim spread out as far as the eye could see. It was a feeling of endless liberation.

"Ahh." She sighed with ecstasy as she rose to ever-greater heights. There was nothing else like this precise moment. It was an exultation that brought one to the verge of tears. Since time immemorial, mankind had dreamed of flying like the birds. Finally, in this virtual world, we had found our own wings.

She hated the system's limits on flight. She wanted to experience it to her heart's content, going as high and far as she dared. She would give anything for it.

That was a shared desire among every player in Alfheim. Whoever reached the legendary city atop the World Tree before the other races would be reborn as an alf, a true fairy—and all flight limits would be repealed. You would be the true ruler of the skies.

Leafa had no interest in powering up her character or earning rare loot. There was only one reason she kept playing the game.

She beat her wings powerfully once more, reaching for the golden moon so far out of her reach. The motes of light falling off her wings fell through the night sky, trailing green tails like tiny comets.

"L-Leafa, wait uuup." The wheedling voice came from below, and she was brought back to reality. Leafa stopped ascending and looked down to see Recon struggling behind her, clutching his controller. Flight with the training stick was severely limited when it came to speed, and Recon stood no chance of keeping up if Leafa flew at her maximum speed.

"Come on, put your back into it!" she urged Recon, beckoning with both hands as she hovered, wings outspread. She scanned the surroundings and found the imposing landmark of the World Tree amid the night, using it to ascertain the direction of sylph territory.

Once Recon had finally reached her altitude, Leafa began gliding easily, matching his speed. He looked over, clearly worried.

"A-are you sure we aren't a little too high?"

"The higher we are, the better it feels. Plus, if your wings get tired, you have plenty of time to glide."

"Have I ever told you that you change when you're flying?"

"Have you ever told me *what*?"

"N-never mind..."

They proceeded onward toward southwest Alfheim, where the sylphs held their own territory, playfully bickering all the while.

They'd been in a party of five today, hunting in a neutral-zone dungeon to the northeast of sylph land. Luckily, they didn't have to contend with any other parties and hunted to their hearts' content. But when they prepared to head for home laden with money and items, they were waylaid by a group of eight salamanders.

Warfare was permitted between races in ALO, but only a small minority of players practiced such banditry. Today's adventure taking place on a weekday afternoon, they hadn't expected to run across any large groups of roving enemies, which made the encounter all the more bitter.

After a pair of air battles on the run, three had fallen on either side, which left Leafa and Recon as the only sylph survivors. They'd made good use of the sylphs' advantageous flying speed, however, and had managed to escape the salamanders' pursuit. Now they were nearly within range of sylph territory. They needed to hide and wait for Recon to recover after the battle, but it seemed they were going to make it out safely. However, on an idle scan of the forest behind them, Leafa saw...

A brief flash of orange light at the foot of a dense cluster of particularly large trees.

"Look out, Recon!" she shouted, and peeled off downward to her left. In the next instant, three fiery shots burst out from the leaves below.

Their extra altitude was fortuitous, as they had just enough extra time to avoid the blazing projectiles. The night air charred around them.

But there was no time to relax. Five reddish shadows emerged out of the stretch of forest that had produced the fireballs, and they sped after Leafa and Recon.

"Ugh, would you just give up already?" she spat, peering to the northwest. She still couldn't see the light of the giant wind tower that marked the center of sylph territory.

"Oh well, we'll just have to fight!" She pulled a gently curved long blade from her waist.

"Not more of this!" Recon wailed, readying his dagger.

"There are five of them, so I don't expect to win, but you'd better not just give up! I'll try to draw their attention, so make sure you beat at least one of them."

"I'll try…"

"You ought to show me you can act heroic once in a while." Leafa jabbed Recon's shoulder, then readied herself to dive. She rounded herself up, did a loop for momentum, and folded in her wings at a sharp angle so that she dropped like a rock. She shot downward at the salamanders' wedge formation with reckless abandon.

Leafa and her party were old hands who'd been playing ALO since the start, with considerable experience and equipment. The only reason they'd suffered such an ignoble defeat was not just the enemy's number but the battle formation that the salamanders had recently begun employing. They sacrificed mobility by wearing heavy armor, and they used their weight as momentum for devastating charging lance attacks, over and over. The array of deadly horizontal spearheads flying forth was so overpowering that it was nearly impossible to use the sylphs' natural agility in battle.

But after their second midair clash earlier, Leafa thought she'd detected a weakness in the enemy's strategy. She summoned blind courage, unhesitatingly diving straight for the figure at the center of the wedge. The gap closed in no time. All of her attention focused on the sharp tip of the enemy's silver lance.

The high-pitched whine of the sylphs' descent and the metallic roar of the salamanders' approach mixed dissonantly as they grew louder, and when the two crossed paths, there was an explosion that shook the air.

Leafa gritted her teeth and evaded the fangs, which were the enemy's deadly lance thrust, with nothing more than a slight inclination of her neck. She ignored the burn of the tip as it grazed her cheek. The next instant, she brought down the long katana from directly overhead, aimed at the enemy's red helmet.

"Seyyy…"

And struck.

"Yaaah!!"

His eyes went wide with shock beneath the thick visor, but before she could process the satisfaction, there was a burst of yellow-green light and a massive tremor through her hands as the enemy flew backward.

His HP bar shot downward, but not even a third of his health was lost thanks to his thick armor. More importantly, however, a shock to the head of that caliber would ensure he'd be out of the fight for precious seconds. Leafa immediately readied herself for the next move.

Right here!!

The weakness in the salamanders' heavy attack was how long it took them to regroup once they'd crossed paths with the target. As soon as she shot past the other four enemies, Leafa twisted hard, wings outstretched, in a sharp left turn.

Her entire body groaned with the hard horizontal g-force, but she withstood it, pushing with her right wing and running control with her left. Soon the enemy line came into view, still in the process of turning to meet her.

Even if the armor-laden salamanders knew her plan, there was no way for them to speed their rotation. She darted forward, sword flashing at their flanks.

Her torso slash caught the leftmost fighter cleanly. Their formation fell apart.

Now I just need to force them into a melee!

Out of the five salamanders, only the leader Leafa had already dispatched was using Voluntary Flight. The others were equipped with controllers, which meant Leafa had a considerable advantage when it came to midair dexterity.

She looked around for Recon and saw him in fierce combat with the rightmost salamander. His demeanor might not have shown it, but he was a veteran player. Once Recon had a foe in close combat, his skill with a dagger shone.

Leafa stuck fast to the rear of her target, meting out constant and significant damage with her long katana. *We might actually win this*, she began to think. The only concern in her mind was the prior blast of fire magic: One of the five must be a mage. They were all in heavy armor, which meant one of them was probably just a spellsword with some secondary magic at his disposal. But backup skills or not, even low-level salamander fire magic packed a serious punch.

Common sense said that the mage would be on the right or left flank, which meant that either Leafa or Recon was dealing with him at this very moment. As tightly as they clung to their opponents, they were keeping either foe from firing off any spells. If they could just take down these two, it would be an even fight from that point on.

"Rahhh!!"

Leafa unleashed another of her patented overhand slices with a bellow. It struck the salamander on the shoulder, tearing another chunk out of his already red HP bar.

"Damn it!" he cursed, and his body was suddenly crimson with flames. The fire roared and ejected tiny red droplets until only a short lick of flame was left floating in the air. This "Remain Light" marked the spot the salamander had died. If a resurrection spell or item was used on it before it died out, he could be instantly brought back to life, but after a minute's time, he would be teleported to his race's home territory to resume play from there.

Leafa immediately banished the fallen foe from her mind and set her sights on the next target. The three remaining were unsure with their giant lances, their movements too slow for close combat. They repeatedly attempted awkward charges, but without any real momentum behind them, it was child's play for Leafa to dart out of the way.

She glanced over again and saw that Recon was going for the finishing blow. He'd lost some HP of his own but not enough to need a healing spell. What had started as a five-on-two air raid was suddenly a very winnable fight. She swung her sword again, emboldened by their odds.

That was when another pillar of fire shot upward from the surface and caught Recon full in the chest.

"Aaaah!" he screamed, stopping in midair.

"No, don't stop!" Leafa shouted, but the nearly dead salamander's lance pierced Recon before he could react.

"I'm sorryyyy…" he wailed as green gusts of wind surrounded his body. The "End Flames" death animation swallowed him whole, and like the last man, he left only a small floating light behind.

Yes, he would come back to life elsewhere in the game in just a matter of seconds, but it never felt good to see a friend fall in battle. Leafa gritted her teeth, but she had no time to mourn his defeat. Another series of flames burst up from below, and she had to make a series of desperate turns to evade.

So the mage was the man at the lead!

If she had known this from the start, she would have followed his fall and finished him off when she had the chance, but it was too late to do anything about it now. The situation was dire.

But she wouldn't give in. She'd struggle until the very last ugly moment, searching for that one blow to land, a philosophy and point of pride she'd earned through years of training as a swordsman.

Two other salamanders who had recovered thanks to the distraction of the magic from below launched another long-range charge.

"Do your worst!" Leafa dared, holding her sword high.

———✦———

"Fmgh!"

After an endless fall, wailing helplessly all the way down, I finally landed somewhere unfamiliar. My cry was stopped short when I came to rest not on my feet but on my face. After several still seconds with my head buried deep in the grass, I slowly rolled over onto my back.

I lay still in the grass for a good long while, savoring the relief that the freefall was finally over.

It was night. Inside a deep forest.

A massive, gnarled tree that could have been centuries old set its impressive branches sprawling in all directions far over my head. Between the leaves I could see black sky littered with stars and a large, golden full moon directly overhead.

Insects buzzed nearby. On top of that, the low song of a night bird. Far-off howls of wild beasts. The scent of plant life tickled my nostrils. A slight breeze caressed my skin. All these sensations pressed in on my senses, terrifyingly vivid. It felt more real than real life—the signature of a virtual world.

I'd been skeptical of Agil's claim, but upon seeing it for myself, I had to admit that the quality of modeling in ALO was in no way inferior to SAO's. Any potential disbelief that someone could create something so incredible in just a year of development was swept away by the sheer volume of information assaulting my senses.

"Well…here I am again," I muttered to myself, eyes closed. Just two months after I was released from my old prison and swore

I'd never do this again, I was back in a full-dive VR world. *Didn't you learn your lesson last time?* a voice in my head accused, and I grimaced wryly.

But this wasn't like the other game. Losing all of my HP wouldn't cause the real me to die, and I could leave at any time... With a start, I realized the path of dark memories that was leading me down.

What was the deal with that strange display error and sudden teleportation? What was I doing in this particular spot? The navigator had said each player would start in his or her chosen race's home city. But this looked like the wilderness.

"Th-this can't be what I think it is..."

Cheek twitching, I lifted my right hand and made a swiping motion with my index and middle fingers, but nothing happened. I tried it a few more times, a cold sweat running down my back, then remembered the tutorial voice saying that menu call-up and the flight controller were used with the left hand.

I tried again with my left this time, and a glowing menu popped up with a pleasing chime. It was virtually the same as the one in SAO. I stared at the buttons listed on the right side.

"Ah, here it is..."

Right at the bottom was a gleaming button labeled LOG OUT. I pressed it just as a test, and a warning message appeared saying that I couldn't log out immediately while in the wilderness, followed by a confirmation prompt.

I sighed in relief, put a hand on the grass, and lifted myself up.

Upon closer examination, I seemed to be smack in the middle of a vast forest. Massive trees towered endlessly in every direction without a light in sight. I still had no idea why I'd landed here of all places, so I decided to check my game map. Just as I was about to press the button, I stopped abruptly.

"Wha...?!" I exclaimed.

At the top of the window was the name "Kirito" and my chosen race of "Spriggan." Below that were my numerical hit points and mana points, reading 400 and 80 respectively—clearly starting values, nothing remarkable.

What startled me was the skill data beneath that. I hadn't chosen anything yet, and I figured that section would be blank, but there were already eight different fields there. They could have been spriggan starter skills, but if that was the case, there seemed to be too many. I touched the list to call up the skill window and examine the details.

The variety was random—from battle skills like One-Handed Swords, Martial Arts, Weapon Defense, to lifestyle skills like Fishing—but the values were extreme. Most of them were leveled to the nine hundreds, and some were at an even thousand with a sign denoting they'd been mastered. MMORPG skills were designed to take an unfathomable amount of time to master, and it was unheard of for them to be maxed out in a new character.

Something was clearly bugged. First that inexplicable teleportation, now this. Maybe the servers were unstable.

"Is there something wrong with this game? I wonder if there's a GM support option…"

I was about to flip through the game's options when something familiar tugged at my brain. I turned back to the skill list. I recognized those proficiency values. One-Sword Skills, 1,000… Martial Arts, 991… Fishing, 643…

It hit me like lightning, so fast it made me gasp.

No wonder I knew these numbers. They were the exact same values I'd earned over two years of constant use in the world of Sword Art Online. Some of them were missing, like Dual Blades—likely because they didn't exist in the world of ALO. In essence, the numbers that stared out at me were the final stats of Kirito the Swordsman as he'd existed in the last moments of the floating castle Aincrad.

My mind roiled. This was impossible. It was an entirely different game run by an entirely different company. Did my save data somehow transfer over? Or, even more unbelievable…

"Am I actually inside SAO?" The words tumbled from my mouth as I sat in the grass.

It took several dozen seconds before I could recover my thoughts. Shaking my head, I forced my brain back into gear and looked at the menu again.

Whatever was happening, I needed more information than what I had now. I checked my inventory this time.

"Oh, geez..."

This time I was greeted by line after line of corrupted text. Random Chinese characters, numbers, and letters were jumbled together in unintelligible strings.

Most likely, this was what remained of my last items in Aincrad. Somehow, I had the old Kirito's data with me.

"Hey...in that case..."

I was struck by a sudden idea.

If my items were still here, that included something extremely valuable to me. I pored over the item text, using my finger to scroll through the menu.

"Please, please carry over..."

The garbled text sped past at high speed. My heart was racing in my chest, clanging like an alarm bell.

"...!"

My fingers stopped of their own accord. Just below them, glowing in a soft lime green, was a string of text reading *MHCP001*.

I forgot to breathe. With a trembling finger, I traced that name. The item was selected and the color inverted. I dragged the item over to the EJECT button.

A white light arose from the surface of the window and quickly concentrated into a tiny object: a colorless, transparent, tear-shaped crystal. There was a softly pulsing glow inside of it.

I carefully cupped the gem with both hands and lifted it up. There was a slight warmth to it. Just that little detail threatened to bring moisture to my eyes.

Please, God, I prayed, tapping the crystal twice with my index finger. Instantly, light exploded in my hands.

"Wha—?"

I stumbled backward. The glowing crystal hovered in the air about six feet off the ground, growing brighter by the second. It shone so powerfully that the trees around me appeared to be white, and the moon above was dim in comparison.

As I watched, wide-eyed, the center of the pulsing vortex of light began to take form. The contours became clearer, and color appeared. I could see long black hair flowing in all directions. A pure white one-piece dress. Slender limbs. A young girl, eyes closed and arms crossed over her chest, gently descended toward the ground, glowing as if she were a personification of light itself.

The explosion disappeared as quickly as it happened, and the girl came to a stop to hover just off the ground. Her long eyelashes trembled and slowly rose as she opened her eyes. Within moments, eyes as deep as the night sky above stared directly into mine.

I couldn't move. Couldn't speak. Couldn't blink.

Her light pink lips slowly cracked into a smile that could only be described as angelic. Emboldened by this response, I finally found my voice.

"Hey, Yui…remember me?"

No sooner were the words out of my mouth than I looked down at myself with a start. My appearance was completely different from the last time she'd seen me. I had no mirror to check for myself, but my clothes and facial features had to be entirely different than before.

But my fear was unfounded. Yui's mouth opened, and her familiar bell-like voice rang out.

"Finally, we meet again, Papa."

Tears glimmering in her eyes, she spread her arms wide and jumped to embrace me.

"Papa…Papa!"

She cried it out over and over, slinging her fragile arms around my neck and nuzzling me with her cheek. I held her small body tight. I could feel a sob leak out of my throat.

Yui. The girl I'd met in the old Sword Art Online world and lived with for just three days before she vanished. It was a short time in the grand scheme of things, but those precious memories were forever burned into my mind. They were the only moments in that long, painful battle in Aincrad that I could honestly say that I was happy.

I don't know how long I stood there holding Yui, feeling a painful sweetness tinged with nostalgia. Miracles were real. I could surely see Asuna again somehow. We could go back to the life we had.

It was the first time I was sure of it since I'd come back to the real world.

"So what the heck is going on here?"

I'd found a stump to sit on, in a corner of the clearing that I'd landed in just a few minutes earlier. Yui was perched cradled on my lap, and I was resisting the impulse to ask her immediately about Asuna.

Yui stopped rubbing her cheek against my chest in sheer bliss long enough to give me a blank look.

"...?"

"We're not actually inside SAO, right...?"

I gave her a brief explanation of what had happened since she disappeared. How I compressed Yui and saved her as client-side data before the server could delete her entirely. How we beat the game and Aincrad was destroyed. How this was a new world, Alfheim, and yet the old Kirito's data was here. The only thing I couldn't put into words was that Asuna still hadn't woken up yet.

"Give me just a moment." Yui shut her eyes, tilting her head slightly as though listening for a voice I couldn't hear.

"I believe this world," she said, her eyes popping open and looking into mine, "is a copy of Sword Art Online's server."

"Copy?"

"Yes. The core program and graphics system are entirely identical. That should be clear from the fact that I'm able to exist in this form. But the Cardinal system's version number is a bit out of date for some reason. Plus the game component resting on top of all that is completely different."

"Hmm…"

I thought hard.

ALfheim Online had been released twelve months after the SAO Incident and not long at all after Argus was shuttered and RCT took over management of its assets. If RCT had absorbed Argus's technological property, it was quite possible for them to essentially re-skin it into a new VRMMO. As long as they hooked everything into the simulation/feedback engine that was the core of the game experience, the development costs would be a fraction of what they might have been if it were created from scratch. It perfectly explained why I thought the world of this game was just as detailed as Sword Art Online's.

So ALO was running off an altered copy of SAO's system. That made sense. But…

"Why would my personal data be here in ALO?"

"Let me take a look at your data first, Papa." She closed her eyes again. "Yes, that settles it. This is your exact same character data from SAO. The formatting is almost entirely the same, so it just overwrote your skill data with the old information. Hit points and mana points are derived from a different equation this time, so they weren't carried over. It seems your items are all corrupted, though. We should get rid of them before you get caught by the error detection protocol."

"I see. Good idea."

I ran my finger across the whole inventory to select all the corrupted items. Some of them were mementos of Aincrad packed with memories, but the situation called for cold pragmatism. Besides, I couldn't possibly pick out and save individual items when their very names were illegible.

I summoned up my will and deleted them in one fell swoop, leaving only my starter equipment behind.

"But what about this skill data?"

"The system has no problem with it. They're unnatural based on your playing time here, but you'll probably be fine as long as a human GM doesn't take a closer look."

"Oh. Okay...I used to be a beater, now I'm just a cheater, I guess."

No problem with my character being high-powered, though. I needed to climb this World Tree and find Asuna—I wasn't looking for a rewarding gameplay experience.

Besides, looking closer at the skill window gave me the sense that a character's numerical data didn't tell the whole story in this game. There was no agility or strength stat like in SAO, and the gains to be made in HP and MP were slight at best. Raising weapon proficiency only unlocked more weapon types to use, and it had no effect on power. And biggest of all, SAO's abundant sword skills were gone.

In other words, ALfheim Online was an action-heavy game in which a player's actual movement and decision-making made the difference, not stats. It would not be like SAO, in which a high-powered character could simply stand still while much weaker foes failed to put a dent into him.

The one major unknown was the existence of magic, which was not a part of SAO. There was an "Illusory Magic" in my skill list—probably a starter skill for spriggans—but I wouldn't know more about how it affected gameplay until I used it...or had it used against me.

Window closed, I had another question for Yui, who was still snuggled against my chest with her eyes shut like a contented cat.

"By the way, how are you handled in this world, Yui?"

She was not actually a human being but an artificial intelligence that broke free of SAO when its mental counseling program bugged out.

In the present day of 2025, several research laboratories had announced the development of their own A.I.s that were extremely close to human intelligence. The ability for programs to act in an intelligent manner had improved to the point that the line between false intelligence and true intelligence was blurring. Those A.I.s that straddled the boundary were some of the most advanced technological feats in existence.

Yui could possibly be counted among them. She might be the very first true artificial intelligence. But none of that mattered to me. I loved Yui, and she adored me. That was enough.

"Let's see. Here in ALfheim Online, it seems they have human-like programs designed for player support, just as in SAO. They're called Navigation Pixies... and that's how I'm categorized."

As she said this, her brow furrowed. A second later, her body glowed and disintegrated.

"What the—?" I shouted in alarm. I was about to leap to my feet and look around when I finally noticed what was resting on my knees.

She was no more than four inches in height. Tiny limbs extended out of a light magenta dress styled like flower petals. There were even two pairs of translucent wings on her back: the very image of a fairy. The size might have been different, but the adorable face and long black hair were unmistakably Yui's.

"This is what I look like as a pixie."

She stood up on my knees, hands on her waist, and flicked her wings back and forth.

"Oooh..."

Impressed, I jabbed her cheek with a finger.

"Hey, that tickles!" She laughed, flitting up into the air with a jingling sound to escape the wrath of my finger, before perching on my shoulder.

"So, do you still have admin privileges like before?"

"No," she said, slightly disappointed. "All I can access are reference data and general map information. I can also view the status of players I've contacted personally, but I can't seem to get into the main database."

"I see. The thing is..." I composed myself to deliver the most important news. "Asuna, your mama... is here in this world."

"Huh...? Mama's here?" She leaped off my shoulder and hovered just in front of my face. "What do you mean?"

"..."

I was about to explain about Sugou but stopped at the last moment. It was the weight of negative human emotions that originally brought Yui to the brink of ruin. I didn't want to expose her to any more malice.

"Even after the SAO server disintegrated, Asuna never came back to reality. I came here on some information that a person who looked like her was spotted in ALO. It could just be a coincidental stranger, but without anything better to go on..."

"I had no idea... I'm sorry, Papa. If I had the authority, I could run a check through the player database and tell you right away, but I don't."

"Actually, I have a good idea where to find her. It's called the World Tree. Do you know where that is?"

"Ah, yes. That would be to the northeast, but it's quite far off. More than thirty miles by real distance."

"Wow, that's really incredible, huh... Five times the diameter of the base floor of Aincrad... By the way, why did I get logged in to such a remote stretch of forest?" I wondered aloud, but Yui didn't seem to have an answer.

"Either your locational data was corrupted or your information got mixed with another player diving within your real-life vicinity. But I couldn't say for sure."

"Would have been nice if I'd been teleported right next to the World Tree. Anyway, I was told you could fly in this game." I got to my feet and craned my neck over my shoulder. "Hey, I've got wings!"

Sprouting from my back were sharply angled, clear gray wings—they almost looked like insect wings. I had no idea how to use them, however.

"So how do you fly?"

"It seems there's a controller for assistance. Put out your left hand and motion like you're gripping something."

Following Yui's instructions, I held out my hand and squeezed. Suddenly, I was holding what looked like a simple joystick.

"Let's see, if you pull it back, you fly up, and pushing it down makes you descend. Turn left or right for rotation, the button accelerates, and letting go decelerates."

"Sounds simple enough."

I tried slowly pulling back the stick. The wings on my back sprung to full extension and began glowing gently. I pulled hard.

"Whoa!"

Abruptly I was floating, gently rising from the forest floor. Once I was a few feet off the ground, my body went into neutral, and I tried pressing the spherical button on the top of the stick. I started gliding forward, smoothly and effortlessly.

After a few experiments with descent and rotation, I started getting the hang of the controls. Compared to the flight-sim VR games I'd tried before, it was actually quite simple.

"Okay, I think I've got it down. Next, I need some basic information. Which way's the nearest town?"

"There's a place called Swilvane to the west. That's the closest—Oh…"

She looked up suddenly.

"What's wrong?"

"Players are approaching. It seems like a group of three chasing one…"

"Ooh, a battle? Let's go check it out."

"You never have a care in the world, do you, Papa?"

I gave Yui's head a quick knuckling, then turned to my inventory to ensure my starter longsword was equipped on my back. I pulled it out and gave a few practice swings.

"Yikes, this thing is so cheap and flimsy. Oh well…"

Once the sword was back in its scabbard, I produced the flight stick again.

"Take the lead, Yui."

"Roger!"

She alighted from my shoulder with a jingling of bells, and I started off on my first flight in the game.

The salamander's gout of magic fire finally hit Leafa square in the back.

"Urgh!!"

There was no pain or heat to it, of course, but it felt as though a giant hand had caught her right in the back, and the shock wave toppled her balance. It didn't do much damage, thanks to the protective wind spell she'd cast during her escape, but sylph territory was still a long way off.

On top of that, Leafa's speed was starting to slow. It was that damned flight limitation. In less than a minute, her wings would lose their power, and she wouldn't be able to fly at all.

"Hngh…"

She gnashed her teeth and dropped into a steep dive for the trees. With the enemy's mage, she wouldn't be able to hide for long, but it wasn't Leafa's style to give up and get hit.

She plunged through the canopy and made her way toward the surface, darting among the many layers of branches, her speed rapidly falling as she did. Eventually, she found a relatively clear space with plenty of thick grass. Leafa made a quick landing, the soles of her boots sliding on the ground to provide traction, and darted for cover around the back of a large tree ahead. Once out of sight, she put her hands in the air to cast a hiding spell.

Just as in fantasy movies, magic in ALO required the chanting of spells out loud. The game system required them to be spoken at a certain volume with clear pronunciation. Any slip of the tongue would cause the spell to fail, and then the caster had to start all over again.

Leafa successfully rattled off the memorized spell as quickly as she could, and a light green vapor issued from around her feet and upward, concealing her from the enemy.

This would protect her for the moment, but a high-level Search skill or clairvoyance spell would quickly see through her disguise. She held her breath and stayed as still as possible.

Within moments, she heard the approaching dull buzz of multiple salamanders. They landed in the clearing behind her. She could hear their measured shouts over the clanking of heavy armor.

"She must be around here somewhere! Search!"

"You know sylphs are good at hiding. We should use magic."

After that, she heard the dull chanting of a spell. She had to hold her tongue to avoid uttering a curse. Just a few seconds later, the rustling of grass being parted came closer and closer.

The small shadows crawling over the massive tree's roots toward her were lizards with red skin and eyes—actual salamanders. They represented the clairvoyance spell in effect. Several dozen searchers spread out in a circle formation from the caster. If they noticed any hidden players or monsters, they would leap out to make contact and burst into flames to alert the caster to the location.

Go away! Try somewhere else! Leafa silently commanded the lizards. They crawled on their paths at random, but her prayer went unheeded. One touched the surface of the vapor concealing her and instantly unleashed a high-pitched cry before lighting into vivid flame.

"There! She's over there!"

Sounds of clanking metal rapidly approached, and Leafa had no choice but to leave the shadow of the tree. She spun around, sword in hand, to see three salamanders facing her with lances at the ready.

"You're a pain in the ass, girl," the man on the right said angrily, raising the visor on his helmet. The man in the center, who seemed to be their leader, continued.

"Sorry, but duty calls. Leave your money and items, and we'll let you go."

"Why? Let's kill her! We haven't had a girl sylph in ages!" the man on the left said this time, also sliding up his visor. The look he gave her was drunk with violence and power.

Her year of experience had taught her that there were more than a few who made a sport of "women-hunting." Leafa's skin crawled with revulsion. Hurling sexist taunts and groping others outside of battle set off the game's antiharassment protection, but killing was central to the game's conceit. Some sick bastards even claimed that killing a female VRMMO player was the greatest pleasure to be found in the game.

It was already bad enough in ALO, which was run with all the proper checks and balances. Leafa couldn't even imagine what happened in that other legendary game without a chill running down her back.

She felt her feet grip the ground and raised her beloved two-handed blade over her head, saving her most powerful glare for the salamanders.

"I'll take at least one of you down with me. Do your worst, if you're not afraid of the death penalty," she growled. The two men on the sides swung their lances, snarling with rage. The leader cut them short with a gesture.

"Give it up. Your wings are at their limit, and we have plenty of stamina to spare."

He was right. Stuck on the ground against a flying enemy was the last place anyone wanted to be in ALO—especially one against three. But she wouldn't give in. Especially not if the alternative was giving them money and begging to be set free.

"You've got a strong will. Very well."

The leader shrugged, raised his lance, and beat his wings so that he hovered off the ground. The salamanders to either side followed his lead, controllers in hand.

Leafa's biceps clenched, preparing to deliver at least one deadly swing at full power, even if it meant she wound up pierced by a trio of spears. They spread out to surround her on three sides. But just as they were set to charge, the scene was interrupted.

The shrub behind them rustled, and a black silhouette emerged. It slipped just past the salamanders, went into some kind of tail-spin, and crashed into the grass with a tremendous clatter.

This wholly unexpected diversion caught Leafa and the salamanders off guard. They all stared at the mystery interloper.

"Ugh, oww... I've got the flying down; it's the landing that's the tricky part."

That carefree comment came from the lightly tanned man who pulled himself off the ground. He had lively spiked hair and large, slightly slanted eyes. The overall combination suggested a rambunctious kid. The clear gray wings on his back marked him as a spriggan.

Leafa couldn't believe her eyes—both that a spriggan would be here, so far from his territory in the distant east, and at the equipment he appeared to be wearing. He was dressed in a simple black doublet and trousers, no armor whatsoever. A flimsy-looking sword was his only weapon. It was clearly starter equipment. What was this newbie thinking, wandering out deep into neutral territory like this?

She called out a warning, unable to stand seeing a clueless newcomer brutally hunted for sport. "What are you doing? Run!"

But the boy in black didn't budge. Did he not realize that PK-ing was legal among the different races? He shoved a hand into his pocket, surveyed the scene of Leafa and the three airborne salamanders, and said, "You need three heavily armed warriors to attack one girl? That's kinda lame."

"What did you say?!" Two of the salamanders took offense to his lazy insult and flew over to flank him, front and back. They lowered their lances and prepared to charge.

"Ugh..."

Even if she wanted to help, Leafa was effectively pinned down by the leader, who was still watching her like a hawk.

"You must be an idiot, barging directly into our business like this. Let's start with you!"

The salamander positioned in front of the boy loudly snapped down his visor. The next moment, his outstretched wings glowed ruby red, and he charged. The one in the rear prepared to charge on a slight delay, so he could catch the boy if he dodged the first attack.

It was a helpless situation for any new player. Leafa bit her lip and averted her eyes, not wanting to see the boy run through...

But something unbelievable happened.

With his right hand still in his pocket, the boy extended his left hand and simply grabbed the deadly tip of the charging lance. The air was shattered by the light and sound of a successful guard effect. As Leafa watched, openmouthed with shock, the boy used the salamander's momentum to hurl him backward, lance and all.

"Aaaah!"

The salamander wailed in surprise as he collided directly with his waiting partner, and they fell to earth with a metallic clatter.

The boy turned around to face them, put his hand on the sword behind his head—and stopped, looking to Leafa hesitantly.

"Um...so am I allowed to waste these guys?"

"I'd say so...That's certainly what they're trying to do to you," she answered, still taken aback by the boy.

"Ah, good point. In that case..."

He pulled the weak-looking sword from its scabbard and let its tip trace along the ground. For all his talk about "wasting" their foes, neither his movement nor his manner suggested much confidence. His weight was balanced much too far forward, with his left foot perched in front, when—

A sudden shock wave erupted where the boy used to be. Even Leafa couldn't follow his path, and she'd never once been caught blind by an attack in the game. She spun around hurriedly to see the boy crouched over, far from where he'd been standing. His pose suggested he'd brought up his sword to slash directly in front of him.

The salamander who was closer to standing after their collision suddenly erupted into red End Flames, then disintegrated. A small wisp of flame was left floating in the air.

How can anyone be so fast? Leafa wondered, terrified. Her body was trembling with the shock of witnessing a move she'd never experienced before.

Only one thing defined a character's movement speed in this world: the speed of the brain when processing the signals sent by the full-dive system. The AmuSphere sent out a pulse; the brain received it, processed it, and then sent feedback in the form of a movement signal. The quicker that response system, the faster a character could move. It was said that only through considerable experience could one eventually move faster than his or her natural reaction speed.

Though she didn't like to toot her own horn, Leafa was one of the very fastest among the sylphs. She'd honed her reflexes over many years, and twelve months of experience in ALO had taught her that no one could get the jump on her in a one-on-one fight. But this shattered that preconception.

As Leafa and the airborne salamander leader watched, stunned, the boy got to his feet and turned around, sword at the ready.

The other remaining salamander was still baffled as to what had happened. He was swiveling around, looking for his foe in the wrong direction.

The boy didn't wait to be found. He prepared another brutal attack, one that Leafa swore she wouldn't miss this time.

His first motion was easy, lazy, unhurried. But as soon as his first step hit the ground—

He blurred as another shock wave ripped the air. She actually saw it this time. It was like watching a movie in fast-forward, unconnected frames burned into her vision. The boy's sword shot from below to above, severing the salamander's torso. Even

the flash of the visual effect was a split second late. He traveled forward a few extra yards and ended with the sword brandished high over his head. Another burst of flame announced a new fatality, and the second salamander was gone.

It was the speed that had originally caught Leafa's eye, and now she belatedly realized what incredible damage he was inflicting. Those two salamanders hadn't been at full HP to start with, but they'd had a comfortable majority of their health remaining. A single blow eliminating them was simply abnormal.

The equation to derive damage in ALO was not very complicated. It only took the weapon's power, hit location, attack speed, and target's armor into consideration. In this case, the weapon damage would be minimal, and the salamanders' armor was formidable. Which meant, by the process of elimination, that this boy's accuracy and speed had to be off the charts.

He raised himself easily to his feet again and set his sights on the salamander leader, still hovering in the air. He rested the sword on his shoulder and asked, "What's up? You want a turn?"

The stunned salamander regained his composure and responded to the boy's matter-of-fact challenge with a pained smirk.

"No, thank you. I know I can't win. If you want my items, I'll leave them for you. My magic skill is nearly at nine hundred—I'd rather not suffer the penalty for dying."

"At least you're honest." The boy grinned. He turned to Leafa. "And how about you, lady? If you want to fight that guy, I won't interfere."

She had to laugh at this display of restraint, given his previous utter lack of it. Suddenly, her determination to take down at least one of the salamanders with her seemed a bit pointless.

"I'll pass. But next time, I'll beat you, salamander."

"Well, I doubt I could beat you one-on-one anyway," the red warrior said, spreading his wings. With a flash of fairy dust, he flew off. A brief rustle of branches sounded overhead, and he disappeared into the black night sky. Only Leafa, the boy dressed in black, and two red Remain Lights were left. Within a minute, both flames were gone.

She turned to the boy, slightly nervous again.

"So...what should I do now? Should I thank you? Run away? Or draw my blade?"

He sliced his sword back and forth quickly before sliding it back into the sheath over his back.

"Personally, given that I'm kind of the heroic knight who saved the princess from the villain in this little scene"—he smirked—"I could go for a tearful, smothering embrace from the grateful princess—"

"What? Are you crazy?!" Leafa screamed, her face suddenly hot. "I'd rather fight you!"

"Ha-ha-ha, I'm just kidding."

She ground her teeth in disgust at his obvious delight, but before she could come up with a snappy retort, a third voice piped up out of nowhere.

"Th-that's right! She can't do that!"

It sounded like a young girl. Leafa looked around the clearing but didn't see anyone. The boy hastened to respond.

"Hey, I told you not to come out!"

Looking closer, she saw something glowing, trying to escape the boy's tunic pocket. It spun free and danced around his face, making petite jingling noises all the while.

"The only ones who get to hug Papa are Mama and me!"

"P-Papa?"

Leafa had to take several steps closer to see that it was a little fairy, small enough to perch on the palm of her hand—a Navigation Pixie, the kind that could be summoned from the help window. But those were only supposed to give prepared answers to basic game questions.

She forgot her suspicion of the boy for a moment and stared at the circling fairy.

"Uh, no, it's not what you—"

He hastily tried to cover the pixie with both hands, smiling nervously. Leafa peered around his hands. "Hey, is this one of those private pixies?"

"Eh?"

"You know! The kind that were given out by lottery to those who preordered the game… Wow! I've never seen one before."

"No, I'm not a—mghf!" the pixie piped up before the boy covered her up again.

"Y-yeah, that. I just got lucky in the draw."

"Hmmm…"

Leafa gave the boy another appraising look, this one from head to toe.

"Wh-what?"

"Just thinking… you're pretty weird. For someone who's been into the game since before it opened, your equipment sure looks starter level. And yet you were super tough back there."

"W-well, I made the account ages ago… but only started playing recently. I was busy with… a different VRMMO."

"Oh?"

This didn't entirely answer her suspicion, but if he'd gotten used to the AmuSphere with a different game, that would at least explain his incredible reflexes.

"But what's a spriggan doing so far out here? Your territory is supposed to be way, way to the east."

"B-because… I got lost…"

"Lost?!" Leafa couldn't help but burst into laughter at his pathetic excuse. "Come on! No one's sense of direction is that bad! You're such a character!"

Now a real belly laugh came bubbling up at his affronted expression. Once she'd had a good chuckle at his expense, Leafa returned her long katana to its sheath.

"Well, I suppose you deserve some recognition. Thanks for saving me. My name's Leafa."

"I'm Kirito, and this is Yui." He spread his hands to reveal the pixie. She bowed and fluttered up to land on his shoulder.

Leafa was somewhat surprised to realize that she actually wanted to sit and talk with this boy named Kirito. It was especially rare for her—she wasn't particularly shy, but she didn't make friends easily in this game. He didn't seem to be a bad person, so she summoned up her courage and asked, "What are you doing after this?"

"Uh, nothing in particular…"

"Oh. In that case…why don't you let me treat you to dinner?"

The boy named Kirito gave her a face-splitting grin. Leafa was inwardly impressed. VR games still hadn't gotten fine emotional simulation down quite right, and few people could make a smile look so natural.

"That'd be great. I'm looking for someone to teach me things."

"About what?"

"About this world. Especially"—he stopped smiling and turned to the northeast—"that tree."

"The World Tree? Sure. Believe it or not, I've got seniority here myself. It'll be a bit of a trip, but I'd recommend going to the neutral town to the north."

"Are you sure? Isn't there a town called Swilvane that's closer?"

Leafa looked at him, exasperated. "True, there is. But you really don't know anything, do you? That's sylph territory."

"Is that a bad thing?" he asked innocently.

She was stunned. "Well, you can't attack any sylphs within a sylph town, but they can attack you."

"Oh, I see…But they're not going to rush out to whack me all at once, are they? You'll be with me, Miss Leafa. Plus, I'd like to see the sylph land; I hear it's beautiful."

"Just 'Leafa' will do. You really *are* weird. Well, if you insist, I don't mind, but…I can't guarantee you'll leave alive," she said, shrugging. She loved the sylph home territory herself, so it didn't hurt to hear him compliment it. She was also drawn to the idea of shocking all of her acquaintances by escorting a rare spriggan around town.

"Okay, I'll fly you to Swilvane. It's about time everyone logs in, anyway."

She checked the window to confirm that it was just past four o'clock in the afternoon. She had a bit of time left to play.

Leafa's wing power was mostly refilled by now; she beat her glowing wings once or twice. Kirito spoke up, curious.

"Wait, you can fly without a controller?"

"Sure I can. How about you?"

"I barely just learned how to use this thing." Kirito made the grasping motion with his left hand.

"Ahh. Well, there's a knack to using Voluntary Flight. Some people pick it up right away; some never figure it out. Let's give it a try, shall we? Turn around and don't pull out the controller."

"Uh, okay."

Kirito gave a half turn, and she extended her index fingers to touch just above the shoulder blades of his slender back. The pixie on his shoulder looked on in curious fascination.

"Can you tell what I'm touching?"

"Yes."

"They call it Voluntary Flight, but you don't just start flying with your imagination. You have to assume that there are virtual bones and muscles sprouting out of this spot, and move them."

"Virtual bones... and muscles..."

He repeated the words vaguely and twitched his shoulder blades. In response, the intangible gray wings sprouting through his black outfit began to tremble with his movement.

"Yes, that's it. First you just want to move all the muscles in your shoulders and back until you get the hang of which ones are connected to your wings!"

As soon as she said that, the boy's back crunched inward. The vibration of his wings rose in pitch until it reached a high-pitched hum.

"Yes, that's the way! Try that again, but harder!"

"Hrrm…"

Kirito tucked in his arms, grunting with the effort. Once she sensed that he'd built up enough thrust, Leafa slapped him heartily on the back.

"Wha—?"

Suddenly, the spriggan shot directly upward like a rocket.

"Aaaaahhh—"

Kirito's wail grew distant as his body got smaller and smaller. A brief rustling of leaves above, and he was already beyond the forest canopy.

"…"

Leafa and the pixie who'd fallen off of Kirito's shoulder looked at each other.

"Uh-oh."

"Papa!!"

They both quickly took to the air after him. Once out of the forest, they scanned the night sky until they noticed an unsteady figure careering left and right against the background of the golden moon.

"Aaaaaahhh…let me oooooofff…"

The piteous wail echoed through the wide, open sky.

"Pfft!"

Leafa and Yui shared another look and burst into laughter together.

"Ha-ha-ha-ha-ha!"

"I-I'm sorry, Papa, this is just too funny!"

They hovered side by side, holding their sides with laughter. When their mirth subsided, a fresh lament from Kirito came floating on the wind, and they fell back into more chuckling.

Legs kicking helplessly, Leafa wondered when she'd last had a laugh as good as this one. Certainly not here in this game.

Once she'd gotten the giggles out of her system, Leafa caught Kirito's collar to halt his wild flight path. She gave him another primer on the knack of Voluntary Flight, and after just a ten-minute lesson, he was already managing to fly unsteadily on his own.

"Whoa...this is...great!" he exclaimed as he tried making wide turns and loop-the-loops.

"Isn't it?" Leafa laughed.

"It's just so...I dunno, *moving*. I wish I could keep flying like this forever..."

"I know!"

In her excitement, Leafa flapped her wings to fly in parallel alongside Kirito.

"No fair! Me, too!" the pixie chirped, taking a spot between them.

"Once you're used to it, practice those back and shoulder blade movements so they're as small as you can make them. If you're too big and sloppy, you won't be able to swing your sword properly during an air battle. Well, are you ready to fly to Swilvane? Follow me!"

She did a tight turn and checked her bearings before setting off for the far side of the forest. She kept her speed low, knowing that it was Kirito's first time, but he soon caught up to her side.

"You can go faster, ya know."

"Oh yeah?" She grinned and folded her wings sharply, picking up her pace. She went faster and faster, hoping to hear Kirito change his tune. The air buffeted her entire body, the wind howling in her ears.

But surprisingly enough, even at 70 percent of her maximum speed, Kirito was following along. Normally, one would slow down well before the actual maximum flight speed designated by the game system, due to the sheer mental pressure. The fact that he could achieve such a range in his first attempt at Voluntary Flight spoke to a very firm willpower.

Leafa gritted her teeth and hit her highest acceleration. She'd never gone this fast with a partner before—nobody else could keep up.

The forest below her was a messy blur. The high-pitched violin whine of sylph flight was blending harmoniously with the whistling woodwind of the spriggan's wings.

"Aaah, I can't take anymooore…"

Yui the pixie zipped back into Kirito's shirt pocket. He and Leafa shared a look, then laughed.

Soon the forest thinned out ahead, and a jumble of different-colored lights came into view. In the center stood a radiant tower, brighter than the rest. They had reached Swilvane, capital of the sylph region, and its iconic Tower of Wind. As they grew closer, the main streets and a variety of players going about their business came into view.

"Hey, there it is," Kirito shouted over the howling of the wind.

"We're going to land at the base of that tower in the center! Uh…wait…" The smile froze on Leafa's face as something occurred to her. "Kirito, do you know how to land…?"

"…"

He froze up as well.

"I do not…"

"Umm…"

The enormous tower already took up half of their field of vision ahead.

"Sorry, too late now. Good luck!" Leafa smiled apologetically and prepared to slow down. She stretched out her wings to catch the air and began the descent to the square, legs held out in front of her.

"Wha…? You've gotta be kidding meeeee—"

The spriggan plunged straight toward the outer wall of the tower, still screaming. Leafa watched him go and said a silent prayer in his honor.

Several seconds later, the air shook with a tremendous crash.

"That was messed up, Leafa…I'm going to be afraid to fly now."

Kirito glared at her vengefully as he sat in the wildly colored flower bed at the base of the jade-green tower.

"I got really dizzy!" exclaimed the pixie on his shoulder, her head swaying in a circle. Leafa leaned over, hands on her hips, trying not to laugh.

"That's what happens when you get too carried away. Consider yourself lucky to have survived at all. I was sure you were dead."

"Gee, thanks for the vote of confidence."

He had slammed face-first into the wall at top speed, but Kirito still had more than half of his HP remaining. He truly was a mysterious newbie. Was he just lucky, or did he know how to brace himself against impact?

"Don't worry, I'll heal you," she reassured him, chanting the healing incantation with her right hand held out to him. Glowing blue dewdrops sprayed out from her palm onto Kirito.

"Oh, cool. So that's magic, huh?" Kirito watched her with intense interest.

"You can't use high-level healing magic unless you're an undine. But the more basic stuff is totally essential, so you ought to learn it."

"So the different races have different magical affinities, huh? What about spriggans?"

"They're good at treasure hunting and illusion magic, I think. Neither of which is very useful in battle, which means they're actually the least popular race."

"Yikes…this is why you should research first," Kirito groaned, getting to his feet. He stretched widely and cast a glance around the area. "Wow, so this is what the sylph town looks like! It's really beautiful."

"Isn't it?" Leafa surveyed her familiar hometown with him.

Swilvane was also known as the "Jade City." Delicate towers were connected by a series of complex midair pathways, and everything in the city shone with one shade of jade green or another. When the entire place was illuminated by the glowing evening lights amid the darkness, the sight was nothing short of pure fantasy. In particular, Leafa believed the splendor of the lord's mansion behind the Tower of Wind was unmatched by any other building in Alfheim.

They both stood in silence, watching people pass through the city of lights, when a voice suddenly called out from the right.

"Leafa! You're all right!"

She turned to see a young sylph with yellow-green hair running up and waving wildly.

"Oh, Recon. Yeah, I'm fine."

He came to a halt in front of Leafa, his eyes shining. "That's just amazing. If anyone could escape from such a large group of enemies, it'd be…uh…"

Recon belatedly noticed the dark figure standing next to Leafa, and he froze for several seconds, his mouth agape.

"Wha…y-you're a spriggan! What are you doing here?" He leaped backward and put a hand on his dagger, but Leafa quickly interceded.

"It's okay, Recon. He saved me."

"Uh…"

She pointed to Recon, who was still confused. "This is Recon, a good friend. He got wasted by those salamanders just before I met you."

"Sorry I didn't get there sooner, then. Hi, I'm Kirito."

"Um, nice to meet you." He grasped Kirito's outstretched hand and bowed deeply. "Wait, no!" Recon leaped backward again. "Are you sure about this, Leafa? What if he's a spy?"

"I had my doubts at first, too. But he seems a bit too airheaded to be a spy."

"Hey, that's messed up!"

Recon watched Leafa and Kirito laugh, suspicion in his eyes, then cleared his throat to get their attention.

"Sigurd and the rest are already sitting down in Daffodil Hall. They're going to divvy up the items there."

"Oh, I see. Umm…"

When killed by an enemy player, any character had a 30 percent chance of his or her equipment being stolen. However, when in a party, insurance slots were available to hold items of particular value. If the player was killed, that item would automatically be transferred to another party member for safekeeping.

Anything of value from the day's hunting party was tagged as insurance, which meant that as the last survivor of the group, Leafa wound up with all the spoils. The salamanders knew that, hence their persistence in chasing her down. Thanks to Kirito, however, she was able to bring the entire haul back to Swilvane.

Normally, the party would rendezvous back in a tavern so that all members, surviving or slain, could redistribute the loot. Leafa considered for a moment before answering Recon.

"I'll pass. None of the items fit my skills, anyway. I'll leave them with you to split up among the others."

"Uh...you're not coming?"

"Nope. I promised Kirito a free meal."

"..."

Now Recon gave Kirito an appraising look of an entirely different sort.

"Don't get any funny ideas, okay?" She gave the toes of Recon's boots a kick, and then opened up a trade window, dumping all of the day's spoils into his inventory. "Just shoot me a message when the next hunt is scheduled, and I'll participate if the time works out. See you later!"

"Um, Leafa..."

But she was growing uncomfortable under the scrutiny. After forcing a premature end to the conversation, Leafa grabbed Kirito's sleeve and pulled him away.

"So was that guy your boyfriend?"

"Was he your lover?"

"Excuse me?!" Leafa tripped on the paving stones at the simultaneous questions from Kirito and Yui. Her wings spread wide as she caught her balance. "No way! He's just a party member!"

"You two seemed pretty close for in-game acquaintances."

"Well, I do know him in real life—he's a classmate at school. But that's it."

"Playing a VRMMO with your classmate, huh? That sounds fun," Kirito said wistfully, but Leafa grimaced.

"It's not all great, actually. Sometimes it reminds you of the homework you need to do."

"Ha-ha-ha, good point."

They made their way down an alley as they chatted. The occasional passing sylph did a double take at Kirito's black hair, but the sight of Leafa accompanying him kept them from voicing any suspicions. Leafa wasn't the most active player in the game, but she was well known around town for winning Swilvane's regular fighting tournaments on multiple occasions.

Eventually, a cozy tavern-inn came into view. It was the Lily of the Valley, a favorite of Leafa's for their excellent dessert selection.

She pushed open the swinging door and surveyed the room finding there were no players inside. In real time, it was early evening, so there would be some time yet before people finished their adventures for the night and came back to celebrate with a drink.

She and Kirito sat down at a window table in the back.

"It's all on me, so order whatever you want."

"In that case…"

"Just don't eat too much, or it'll be rough after logging out," Leafa said, eyeing the tempting dessert menu.

Mysteriously enough, the virtual feeling of fullness after eating a meal in Alfheim did not disappear for a while once out of the game. The ability to eat all the sweets she could stand without worrying about calories was one of the biggest draws of a VRMMO for Leafa. The downside was her mother's scolding when she showed up for dinner without an appetite.

It wasn't uncommon to see news articles about people suffering from malnutrition because they used the system as a dieting aid. Even worse were the heavy players who spent their entire lives in the game and starved to death because the in-game food tricked them into forgetting to eat.

Leafa ordered a fruit bavarois, Kirito a nut tart, and Yui a cheese cookie, to Leafa's surprise. For drinks, they had a bottle of spiced wine. The NPC waitress set their orders on the table as soon as they'd placed them.

"Well, let's make it official: Thanks for saving me."

They clinked their glasses of odd green wine, and Leafa threw the cold liquid down her parched throat. Kirito refilled her glass just as quickly and grinned at her.

"Eh, it just happened that way... Those guys sure were eager for that fight, though. Do you get lots of those PK gangs here?"

"Well, salamanders and sylphs are at odds to begin with. Our territories are adjacent, so there's constant clashing in the hunting grounds between us, and there's been lots of competition for power. It's only recently that there have been organized PKs like that, though. I'm pretty sure they must be planning an assault on the World Tree soon..."

"Speaking of which, I need you to teach me about the World Tree."

"That's right, you mentioned that. But why?"

"I want to get to the top of it."

She gave him an exasperated look. But he wasn't joking—his black eyes were shining earnestly.

"Well...that's what every player in the game wants to do. In fact, it's the greatest quest in the game of ALfheim Online."

"Meaning?"

"You know about the flight limits, right? Every race in the game can only fly for about ten minutes at a time, max. But whichever race reaches the floating city atop the World Tree first—and meets Fairy King Oberon—will all be reborn as a new, higher race called alfs. After that, you'll be able to fly as long and far as you want."

"I see," Kirito murmured, taking a bite of his nut tart. "It's an enticing story. Does anyone know the way to get to the top of the tree?"

"Within the roots beneath the tree is a giant dome. There's an entrance in the roof of the dome that lets you climb up the inside of the tree, but the NPC guardians that watch over the dome are superpowerful. A bunch of the different races have tried to challenge them, but we've been wiped out every time. The salamanders are the most powerful race at the moment. They're probably mustering forces now, gathering money for equipment and items, thinking the next time's the charm."

"So these guardians are that strong, huh?"

"It's insane. ALO opened a year ago. What game has a quest you can't beat even after a year of play?"

"Good point..."

"Well, last autumn, one of the major ALO fan sites started a petition to have RCT rebalance the quest."

"Oh, really? And...?"

"They gave us this canned response. 'The game is properly balanced according to the team's specifications.' Lately, a lot of people are saying that our current strategy is never going to work."

"Could it be that a major story quest's been missed, or that it's simply impossible for a single race to conquer on its own?"

Leafa was about to put another spoonful of bavarois in her mouth but stopped to give Kirito a surprised look. "That's a very sharp idea. As it happens, that's what we're doing now—checking around to make sure we haven't missed any quests. But if it's the latter, that'll never happen."

"Never?"

"I mean, it's a contradiction. The quest is only beatable by the first race to complete it. Who's going to help another race complete the quest if it just means losing out on the prize?"

"So you're saying...the World Tree is essentially impossible to climb...?"

"In my opinion. I mean, there are other quests, and you can always raise your crafting skills...But it's hard to give up on it once you've learned how fun it is to fly...Still, I'm sure we'll get it someday, even if it takes a hundred years..."

"That'll be too late!" Kirito muttered darkly.

Leafa looked up with a start and saw a deep furrow in his brow, his lips twisted as he gritted his teeth in frustration.

"Papa...?" The pixie put down the cookie she'd been holding two-handed and flew over to land on Kirito's shoulder. She rubbed a tiny hand on the boy's cheek to comfort him. A few moments later, he slumped down in resignation.

"I'm sorry to startle you," he said quietly. "I have to get to the top of that tree."

Kirito stared right into her, his eyes as sharp and shining as a finely honed blade. Leafa suddenly realized that her heart had begun to beat much faster. She took a quick sip of wine to hide her fluster.

"Why is it...so urgent?"

"I'm...looking for someone."

"What do you mean?"

"It's hard to explain..."

He gave her a weak smile. But his eyes seemed to be hiding a deep pool of despair. They were eyes that she'd seen somewhere before.

"Well...thanks for the grub, Leafa. I appreciate all the advice. I'm glad you were the first person I ran into." He made to get up, but Leafa unconsciously reached out to grab his arm.

"W-wait. Are you going...to the World Tree?"

"Yeah. I need to see it for myself."

"That would be reckless of you...It's so incredibly far, and there are tough monsters on the way. I can tell you're strong, but..." And before she could stop herself, the words tumbled out of her mouth. "Tell you what. I'll take you there."

"Huh...?" Kirito's eyes grew wide. "No, I couldn't ask you to do that. Not when we just met..."

"It's fine! I've made up my mind!"

Leafa turned her face away to hide the blush that had snuck over her cheeks. Because everyone in ALO had wings, there was no fast-travel system. The trip to Alne, the city at the center of Alfheim that sat around the World Tree, was equivalent to a real-life journey. The offer she'd just made, to this boy she'd met just a few hours before, was simply unfathomable.

But...she just couldn't let him go alone.

"Will you be on tomorrow?"

"Uh, yeah."

"Meet here at three o'clock PM, then. I've got to leave for now. Go to the inn upstairs to log out. See you tomorrow!"

Before she had even finished speaking, Leafa was waving her hand to bring up the game menu. She could log out instantly anywhere in sylph territory, so she smacked the button at once.

"H-hey, wait!" Kirito blurted out, and she looked up to see him smiling at her. "Thanks."

She did her best to smile back, and then nodded before hitting the OK button. The world flashed into a rainbow of light, then blacked out. The sensations of Leafa's body faded away, until only the burning of her cheeks and racing of her heart remained.

Her eyes opened slowly.

The first thing she saw was the familiar ceiling of her room and the large poster she'd pinned to it. It was a custom-made poster of an in-game screenshot blown up as large as she could get it. The picture was of a flying fairy with a long ponytail in the midst of a flock of birds and endless blue sky.

Suguha Kirigaya raised her hands and slowly removed the AmuSphere. The device was two simple rings in a crown-like structure: much more fragile than the original NerveGear but without the same sensation of being clamped into place.

Even back in the real world, her cheeks were still ablaze. She sat up in bed, slapped her face, and raised a silent wail inside her chest.

Aaaahhh!

Waves of belated embarrassment crashed over her at her boldness. Recon (her classmate Shinichi Nagata) once said that when Suguha was Leafa, she was at least 50 percent bolder. Today's escapade was well above that mark. She writhed in agony, her legs flopping on the bed.

He was such a strange boy. Well, there was no saying whether the player was actually a boy, but Suguha's instinct told her he was quite close to her age. But between his relaxed demeanor and his occasional mischievous remarks, it was hard to tell for sure.

His personality wasn't the only mystery, though. Where did that incredible strength come from? In her year of playing ALO, he was the first person she'd come across who didn't seem beatable in a duel. She spoke his name very quietly.

"Kirito, huh...?"

The first time that Suguha had felt the urge to see a virtual world for herself was just about a year after the SAO Incident began.

Until then, the concept of a VRMMO was nothing but a target of loathing to her, the tool that had literally stolen her brother from her. But the more she held Kazuto's hand as he slept in his hospital bed, the more she spoke to his deaf ears, the more she began to wonder what his world was like. It was up to her to bridge the distance that was now between them, she had thought.

Midori had given her a long, hard look when Suguha said she wanted an AmuSphere, but she eventually granted her daughter's request, asking only that she be mindful of the time and her health.

The next day at lunch, Suguha visited the desk of Shinichi Nagata, the biggest gamer in class—for better or for worse—and asked him to come up to the roof with her to discuss a serious topic. The absolute silence and subsequent frenzy of the class after this scene was still the stuff of legend.

Leaning against the chain-link fence around the roof, Suguha asked the hopelessly anticipatory Nagata to teach her about VRMMOs. After several seconds and an entire emotional spectrum of facial expressions, he asked her what kind of game she had in mind.

When Suguha told him that she couldn't take any time away from her studies and kendo practice, Nagata pushed his glasses up on his nose and muttered some gibberish like, "You'll want a skill-based entry rather than a grindfest time-sink, then." Ultimately, his best recommendation was ALfheim Online.

She hadn't been expecting him to start playing ALO with her, but with the help of his thorough tutorials, Suguha found that she was surprisingly well suited to this virtual world game. There were two main reasons.

First, Suguha's years of diligent kendo study translated extremely well into the game.

When players squared off in battle, evasion was a foreign concept. It was a foregone conclusion that both sides would hit the other; as long as your total damage was higher, the battle was won. But Suguha's well-trained reflexes and instincts meant she could easily avoid most attacks. In a way, her almost unfair skill at the game was a natural outcome.

If ALO had been a level-based MMO like so many others, the lack of time to invest in her character meant she would never match the core players. In fact, among the veterans of ALO, Leafa's stats were actually below average. It was only because ALO was such a skill-based game that she was powerful enough to be considered one of the Five Great Sylphs.

The second thing that drew Suguha to the game was something entirely unique to ALO: the flight system.

She could still easily remember the sensation of absolute joy the first time she got the knack of Voluntary Flight and was able to fly of her own free will.

Suguha was small. Her lack of reach in kendo bouts was a constant thorn in her side, and as a response, she had learned from a young age to always go faster, farther. So the way that ALO let her use that long katana in an overhead stance—impossible when one hand was holding a flight stick—and then slash through foes at extreme long range was bliss beyond compare. And beyond that, there were the sharp dives that threatened to shake her to pieces; the long, gentle cruises at high elevation among the flocks of birds; and so much more. With the act of flying, Suguha was deeply in love.

So while slow, clumsy Recon called her a "raging speedaholic," Suguha couldn't imagine playing ALO without the joy of flight.

After a year of experience in the game, Suguha was a fully dedicated VRMMO player. She'd started this experiment to grow closer to her brother, and now she loved it for what it was.

Several times a day since Kazuto had come back, Suguha had desperately wanted to talk to him about ALO—to share the pains and pleasures of the virtual world she'd finally come to understand with him. But the sight of the shadows behind his eyes kept her from ever broaching the subject.

She was certain that even after the horrors of the SAO Incident, Kazuto still loved the idea of a virtual world. All the NerveGears were supposedly recalled, but he'd gotten his back somehow, and the Sword Art Online ROM card was stuck in the photo stand on his desk.

But the SAO Incident wasn't over for Kazuto. Not until *she* woke up.

The thought tore Suguha's heart to pieces. She never wanted to see him cry in such terrible despair again, the way he had last night. She wanted him to have a smile on his face at all times. And for that reason, she wanted his lost love to wake up.

But she knew that when it happened, Kazuto's heart would be forever beyond her reach.

If only they'd been actual siblings. She'd never have come to feel this way. She'd never desire to keep Kazuto all to herself.

As she lay back in bed and stared at the poster of the Alfheim sky, Suguha wondered why people didn't have wings. She wished she could fly as far as she wanted in the real sky, until the tangled web around her heart was blown away.

I stared at the seat that had held the sylph girl named Leafa just moments before, still a bit shaken.

"I wonder what got into her," I muttered. On my shoulder, I could feel Yui tilting her head in confusion.

"I don't know...I don't have my old mental monitoring functions anymore."

"Figures. Well, it's nice of her to offer to show me the way."

"If a map is what you need, I've got one. But the more on our side, the safer we'll be. On the other hand..." Yui stood up to speak directly into my ear. "You shouldn't cheat on Mama, Papa."

"I'm not, I'm not!"

I shook my head furiously. Yui leaped off my shoulder with a giggle and landed on the table, resuming her two-handed cookie feast.

"Sure, it's all funny to you," I grumbled, taking a swig directly from the bottle of herb wine.

She had a point, though. Not about "cheating" on anyone, but the simple fact that Leafa wasn't just a character in a game. There was a player on the other end, a stranger with an entirely different personality.

For a very long time, the virtual world had been my reality. It was pointless to ponder the differences between player and character there—all emotion, whether malicious or friendly, was real. It was the only way to survive.

But that didn't apply here, of course. All players were acting out a persona; the only differences were in the degree. There was no stigma against playing as a thief—attacking, stealing, killing; if anything, it was recommended.

"This VRMMO stuff is tricky." I sighed, then grimaced at my words. I put down the empty bottle and dropped Yui—still challenging the cookie as big as she was—onto my shoulder. It was time to leave this world for a bit.

The particulars of logging out in an MMORPG were a delicate balance between player convenience and game fairness.

For example, there were many times when one needed to leave abruptly to handle a pressing personal matter or attend to physical needs, which was fine. But if logging out were instantaneous across the board, what was to stop a player from abusing the feature in the midst of a losing battle or during a chase after committing theft? Most MMORPGs therefore placed limits on logging out. ALO was no exception: instant log-out was only possible in one's own territory. Anywhere else, and the player's soulless avatar was left in place for several minutes, openly susceptible to attack or theft.

Logging out of the game safely outside of racial territory required the use of a special camping gear item or taking out a room at an inn, so I decided to follow Leafa's advice and leave the game from the second floor of the Lily of the Valley.

I checked in at the counter and climbed the stairs. Behind the door with the number I'd been given was a simple room with just a bed and table. I was struck by a powerful sense of déjà vu. Until I'd earned enough money to buy my own room in Aincrad, I'd stayed many a night in rooms like this.

All I needed to do was open my window and hit the log-out button, but I decided to remove my equipment and lie down in bed to try a "sleep log-out."

There was one other issue with logging out, specific to full-dive VR games. If the signals from the virtual in-game senses and the real senses were too different over the short interval of leaving the game, an unpleasant dizziness could result. For example, going from a standing position to sitting could cause a brief lightheadedness. Before I ever played SAO, I'd tried a flight game and logged out during a severe nosedive. Even after recovering my normal senses, I was plagued by the sensation of falling for some time, an experience I had no desire to repeat.

The ideal solution to this issue was called a "sleep log-out," which was to enter sleep inside the virtual world, log out automatically, and wake up from sleep in the real world.

I sprawled leisurely on the bed and watched as Yui finished her cookie and came flapping over. She spun around once and landed on the floor in her original form. Her long hair and white dress rippled, and a whiff of perfume floated on the air.

Yui pulled her arms behind her back, leaned forward slightly, and said, "Good-bye until tomorrow, Papa."

"I guess you're right. Sorry, Yui. You waited so long to see me again... I'll be right back for you, okay?"

"Umm..."

She cast her eyes down, her cheeks reddening slightly. "Can I lie on the bed with you until you log out?"

"Huh?"

An embarrassed smile floated onto my face. I was nothing but Yui's "papa," and she was simply an AI seeking a greater range of data from her surroundings, but she also took the form of a very cute girl, and her words were enough to make me feel self-conscious...

"Uh, yeah. Sure."

I had to suppress my shyness and roll toward the wall to give Yui room. She smiled happily and hopped onto the bed.

As she rubbed her cheek against my chest and I stroked her long hair, I murmured, "We need to rescue Asuna quickly so we can buy another home somewhere. Do you think there are player homes in this game?"

Yui looked surprised for a moment, then nodded. "They seem to be quite expensive, but they're available." She paused. "It would be like a dream, wouldn't it, you and me and Mama, to live as a family again. Just the three of us..."

Nostalgia gripped my chest like a vise as I remembered those fond days. It was only a few months ago, but it seemed like a product of the long-distant past, never to be regained...

I hugged Yui tight and closed my eyes.

"It's not a dream... I'll make it real soon enough..."

I was suddenly struck by a deep sleepiness, perhaps after the mental rigor of my first dive in quite a while.

"Good night, Papa." Yui's voice rang like a dainty bell, caressing my mind as I sank into the warm darkness of sleep.

3

The pair of birds spread their wings on top of the white table, chirping morning songs.

She held out her hand. As soon as her finger traced down the brilliant jasper, the birds took flight without a sound. They danced up in an arc and spun off in the direction of the light.

She stood from the chair and followed them for several steps. But before very long, the thin golden bars blocked her path. The birds flitted through the gaps into the outside air—higher, higher, and off into the distance...

Asuna stood in that spot for several moments, until the birds had melted into the color of the sky, and then slowly turned on her heel back to the chair.

The round table and chair were made of white granite, chilly and hard. To the side was a magnificent covered bed, also pure white. Those were the only items in the room...if you could call it a room.

It was perfectly round, with enough space to take twenty steps across the—you guessed it, perfectly white—tiles before reaching the gleaming metallic bars. The space between the bars was just wide enough that Asuna could have squeezed through if she tried, but the system prevented her from doing so.

The intersecting golden bars stretched vertically before meshing together overhead in a dome. At the top was an enormous ring with a frightfully large branch running through it that supported the entire massive structure. The knobby, winding bough cut through the view above until it joined the trunk of the gigantic tree, so large it blotted out a section of the otherwise endless sky.

Which made this room a giant golden birdcage, hanging from the branch of an impossibly large tree—but no, that description wasn't right. The birds who came to visit could come and go freely between the metal bars. It was a cell designed to hold a single prisoner: Asuna.

A fragile, elegant, beautiful, but cruel cell.

Sixty days had already passed since Asuna woke up here, but she wasn't sure of that number. There was no way to write down the count, so she had to remember it herself. On top of that, the game did not run on a full twenty-four-hour clock, so even if she slept and woke based on her body's circadian rhythm, the mornings and nights didn't match up.

Every time she woke, she told herself what day it was, but she was losing confidence in her number. What if she was just repeating the same day over and over? What if she'd already spent years in here? The more she fell into the haze of confusion, the further back in her memory slipped those precious days she'd spent with Him.

The last moment they'd been together...

As the floating castle Aincrad had crumbled into dust and the world melted into light and nothingness around them, Asuna had held him close, waiting for the moment it all ended.

She'd had no fear. She'd known that she'd done what she must and lived the life that she needed to live. She was almost happy to die, as long as it was with him.

The light had enveloped them, their flesh disappeared, their souls intertwined, and they had flown up, up, up...

Then his warmth was gone. In an instant, it was dark all around. She'd reached out desperately, calling his name. But the cruel, relentless current had grabbed her, pulling her away through the darkness. There were intermittent flashes of light. When she felt she was being taken somewhere unfamiliar, she'd screamed. Eventually, a spray of rainbow light had swelled in front of her, and she'd plunged through it—to land in this place.

The wall that supported the gothic canopy over the bed also held a large mirror. The person she saw in it was slightly different from before. Her face and long, chestnut-brown hair were the same. But she was dressed in an uncomfortably sheer one-piece white dress. There was a ribbon red as blood adorning the breast. Her bare feet were cold against the chilly stone tiles. She had no weapons to speak of, but there were strange transparent wings on her back. They were closer to an insect's wings than a bird's.

At first, she thought she was in the land of the dead. But now she knew that was not the case. There might not be a game window when she waved her hand, but this was clearly another virtual world apart from Aincrad. It was a digital prison created by a computer. And she was being held against her will by an act of human malice.

Which meant she could not give in. She couldn't submit and crumble before evil. So Asuna bore the terrible loneliness and impatience that hounded her every day. Even that was becoming more and more difficult, however. She could feel the poison of despair slowly tainting her heart.

She sat on the cold chair, folded her hands on top of the table, and, as she always did, said a silent prayer to Him.

Hurry... Hurry and come save me, Kirito...

"That's the loveliest look on your face, Titania," the voice said, echoing through the birdcage. "The look right before you burst into tears. I wish I could freeze it and put it on display."

"Why don't you do it, then?" she answered, turning to face the voice.

On the side of the cage that faced the World Tree was a small door. A smaller branch running off the large one extended to the door, stairs carved along its length.

A tall man was entering through that doorway.

He had wavy locks of rich golden hair, with a crown of platinum around his brow. There were wings like Asuna's on his back, but they were more like a butterfly's than translucent. They were as lustrous as black velvet, with brilliant emerald-green patterns running across them.

His face was so perfectly elegant that it screamed artificiality. A shapely nose extended down from his smooth forehead, and his long, slender eyes glimmered with the same green color of his wings. The illusion of beauty was ruined only by the sneer plastered on his narrow lips. It was twisted and spiteful.

Asuna looked at him for an instant before turning away, as if avoiding an unpleasant sight. She spoke flatly, without inflection or emotion.

"You're the system admin; it's well within your power."

"Why must you be so cold, my dear Titania? Have I ever placed my hands on you against your will?"

"Does it matter? You've locked me in here. And stop calling me by that stupid name. I'm Asuna, Oberon...I mean, Mr. Sugou."

Asuna looked again at the face of the Fairy King Oberon, the avatar of Nobuyuki Sugou. She did not avert her glance this time. She gave him the full brunt of her gaze.

His mouth twisted in distaste as he spat, "How very unenchanting. In this world, I am Oberon, King of the Fairies, and you are Titania, my queen. We are the rulers of Alfheim, the object of envy to every player in the game. Isn't that good enough for you? When will you open your heart to me and be my proper partner?"

"You will be waiting until the end of your days. All I feel for you is scorn and disgust."

"How headstrong of you." He smirked with one cheek again and then stretched out a hand to Asuna's face.

"But these days I wonder..."

She tried to turn away, but he caught her under the chin and pulled her face straight toward him.

"... if it might be more fun just to take you by force."

Asuna's head was fixed in place as though by an unseen omnipotence. The fingers of his left hand snaked forward to touch her. From cheek to lips, his slender fingers lingered on her skin. The somehow slimy sensation of his otherwise-clean fingers sent a chill down her spine.

In her disgust, she shut her eyes and clenched her teeth. After several rubs of her lips, Oberon ran his fingers down the nape of her neck. In time, they arrived at the red ribbon tied just over her cleavage. He tugged ever so slightly at the end of the ribbon—once, twice—as if enjoying her shame and fear.

"Stop," she said hoarsely, unable to bear it.

Oberon chuckled, deep in his throat, and released the ribbon. He pulled his hand away and waggled his fingers, his voice mirthful.

"I'm only joking. I said I wouldn't take you against your will, didn't I? You'll come around to me soon enough. It's only a matter of time."

"If that's what you think, you're truly insane."

"Ha-ha! You won't be singing that tune for long. Very soon, I will control your emotions in the palm of my hand. Look, Titania." Oberon placed both hands on the table and leaned over it. He swiveled his head around the birdcage, leering widely. "Can you see them? Thousands and thousands of players, diving into this expansive world, enjoying the game. The thing is... none of them has any idea that the full-dive system isn't just a tool for mere entertainment!"

Asuna's mouth clamped shut at these unexpected words. Oberon spread his arms theatrically.

"Of course it's more than that! This game is nothing but a

by-product. The NerveGear and AmuSphere, these full-dive interfaces, focus their electron pulses into very limited regions of the brain's sensory regions, meaning that we're only providing them with virtual environment signals. But…what would happen if those shackles were released?"

There was a dangerous, unhinged gleam in Oberon's wide, emerald-green eyes. Asuna felt an instinctual fear grip her insides.

"It means we can access much more than the brain's sensory fields. Thought, emotion, memory: We can control all of it!"

Asuna could find no response to the madness of his statement. She had to take several breaths before any words came to her lips.

"But no…you can't get away with that…"

"Who's going to say no? Research is advancing in several countries around the world. The problem is, what the research really needs is human subjects. After all, one must be able to put their thoughts into words for us to understand them!"

He practically leaped from the table, cackling in high tones, striding in circles around Asuna as he spoke.

"And there is great variety in higher brain function among individuals, which necessitates a great number of subjects. However, this is *the brain* we're tinkering with. One cannot snap one's fingers and obtain human test subjects. Which means human progress in this field has been woefully slow. But then…what should I see when I'm watching the news but a story about ten thousand ideal test materials!"

Asuna's skin crawled again. Finally, she could see where Oberon was taking this.

"Mr. Kayaba was a genius, but he was also a fool. How could he utilize that incredible potential just to create a stupid game? I couldn't touch the SAO server itself, but it was quite easy to tamper with the router such that when the players were released, I was able to seize a number of them before they got away."

The fairy king made a large cup with his hands, running his tongue over them as though savoring an invisible liquid.

"Oh, how I waited for that damnable game to be beaten! I didn't get all of them, but I did get a good three hundred, at least. Certainly more than any real hospital or laboratory could hold. Long live the virtual world!" he ranted, the heat of his delusions driving him to a soliloquy of madness. She had always hated this tendency of his.

"Thanks to you former SAO players, my research has progressed in leaps and bounds in only two months! I've embedded brand-new artificial implants within human memory and, in doing so, succeeded in creating a rudimentary form of direct emotional control. How fabulous it feels to control the human soul!"

"You can't... You won't get away with this. Father will never let you continue such mad research."

"He will if he doesn't know a thing about it, of course. The project has been undertaken in absolute secret, with a tiny team answering directly to me. We can't commercialize it otherwise."

"Commercial...?"

"There's a major business in America eagerly awaiting our results. We're going to make a fortune selling them the research—along with RCT itself, at some point."

"..."

"Soon I'll be a member of the Yuuki family. I'll only be a son-in-law at first, but eventually I will be the rightful heir to RCT in name and fact. With you as my wife. So what's the harm in doing some dress rehearsals in preparation for the big day in real life?"

Asuna stifled the shivers running up and down her back, and then shook her head quickly but firmly.

"No... you can't. I won't let you do this. Once I get back to the real world, I'll expose all of your wicked deeds. The world will know."

"Oh, come now. You still don't get it? The only reason I told you about the experiment is because you'll be forgetting everything right away. And all that will remain is your devotion to..."

Oberon stopped talking mid-sentence, his head cocked in silence. He held up his hand and opened a game window, then spoke into it.

"I'm coming. Wait for orders." He closed the window and resumed his leer with a soft purr. "I hope my point has sunk in by now: You are going to love and serve me with a blind, devoted passion. But naturally, I have no desire to use your brain as my first test subject. So I'll be praying that you are already more subservient at our next meeting, Titania."

He gave her hair one last stroke before turning to leave.

Asuna did not watch him as he strode across to the door. She was too busy steeling her heart against the terror that his final words commanded.

The door clanked shut heavily, and silence returned.

—◇◇◇—

Suguha left the kendo club, back in her school uniform, bamboo *shinai* case slung over her shoulder. The breeze through the school's valley brushed her cheek comfortably.

It was one thirty in the afternoon, and with fifth period already in progress, the campus was quiet. The first- and second-year students were in class, and any third-years who elected to come to school were in special focused seminars to prepare for high school entrance exams. Only the students with advancement recommendations already in place, like Suguha, were free to stroll around the grounds at this hour.

She felt at ease, but Suguha didn't like coming to school just to hang out. If she came across a classmate, there was guaranteed to be a sardonic comment or two directed her way. But the school's kendo club advisor was very dedicated and couldn't stand to be out of the loop with his favorite pupil heading off to join a kendo powerhouse high school. As a result, Suguha had been ordered to visit the school dojo once every day.

According to him, Suguha's blade had picked up an eccentricity recently. Secretly, Suguha shrugged it off and agreed with him. Nearly every day, she was spending at least some amount of time in Alfheim, mixing it up in wild aerial battles without a hint of proper form or discipline.

Fortunately, this hadn't had an effect on Suguha's ability as far as the kendo club was concerned. Just today, she had scored two consecutive points on the club adviser, a man in his thirties who had once ranked highly in the national tournament himself. She was rather proud of her victory.

Lately, she found it particularly easy to see the opponent's strikes. When locked in battle with a powerful foe, she felt her nerves stretching to their limit, and it was almost as though time itself slowed down.

She thought back to her match with Kazuto a few days prior. She had given him her best shot multiple times, and he'd evaded every one. His reaction speed was so fast, it was almost as though he sensed time on a different scale. It made her wonder: What if the experiences during a full dive had some kind of effect on one's real body upon returning...?

Suguha was idly walking toward the bicycle rack, lost in thought, when a voice called out from the shadow of the school building.

"...Leafa."

"Aah!"

She was so startled that she jumped back a step. It was a scrawny boy with glasses. Those sagging, hangdog eyebrows that he shared with Recon were even droopier than normal.

Suguha put her hand on her hip, exasperated. "Didn't I tell you not to call me that at school?"

"S-sorry...Suguha."

"Why, you..."

She put a hand on her *shinai* case and took a threatening step. He panicked, a terrified smile frozen on his face.

"S-s-sorry! I mean Kirigaya."

"...What is it, *Nagata*?"

"I-I have something to tell you...Can we find someplace more comfortable to talk?"

"You can tell me here."

Shinichi Nagata slumped his shoulders, looking pathetic.

"...In fact, you already have a recommendation for high school. What are you doing here?"

"Um, I've been here all day. I needed to tell you this, Su... Kirigaya."

"Ugh! Don't you have anything better to do with your time?" Suguha took several more steps backward until she could sit down on the tall edge of the flowerbed. "So, what is it?"

Nagata sat down next to her at an awkward distance and said, "Sigurd decided we should go hunting again this afternoon. They want to hit up an underwater cave. Plus, there won't be much concern about salamanders there."

"I told you to text me news about hunts. Sorry...but I'm not participating for a while."

"Huh? How come?"

"I've got to go to Alne..."

In the center of Alfheim, there was a large neutral city at the foot of the massive World Tree. That was Alne. Not only was it quite a long distance from Swilvane, but there were several points along the journey that were impossible to fly over. It would take several days to make the trip.

He stared at her in openmouthed disappointment for several moments, then sidled closer. "Y-you mean you're still working with that spriggan...?"

"Yeah, pretty much. I'm acting as his guide."

"W-what are you thinking, Lea—Su—Kirigaya?! Y-you can't spend the night with that weird stranger..."

"Why are you blushing? Stop imagining me in stupid situations!"

She whacked him on the chest with her *shinai* case. He stared at her with open resentment, his eyebrows at perfect forty-five-degree angles.

"When I suggested going to Alne earlier, you totally brushed me off…"

"Because we'd be flattened over and over if I was with you! Anyway, that's what I'm doing, so let Sigurd and the others know."

She hopped up, briefly waved good-bye, and took off at a trot for the bicycle rack. His scolded-puppy look needled at her heart, but there were already rumors floating around them at school. She had no desire to close that distance with him.

I'm only escorting him there. That's all.

She repeated the words over and over, trying to convince herself they were true. But every time she thought of Kirito and his mysterious black eyes, she couldn't contain her fidgeting.

Suguha quickly undid the lock on her bike, parked in the corner of the large bicycle area. She swung a leg over the seat and took off, pedaling at a stand. The winter air was prickly on her cheeks, but she paid it no mind. Out the back gate she went, then raced down the steep hill without using her brakes.

I just want to fly, she told herself. The thought of another breathless parallel flight with Kirito, at top speed, set her heart racing.

She made it home just before two.

Kazuto's bicycle wasn't in the backyard. He must still have been at the gym.

He'd basically recovered the build he had before the SAO Incident, but that was apparently not enough. He still felt a difference between his real self and his virtual self.

That was natural. It was impossible to make one's body capable of the same things as a virtual avatar—but she understood how he felt. More than a few times, Suguha had felt that urge to fly in real life and nearly fallen off her bike.

She entered the house through the yard, tossed her kendo *dogi* into the washing machine, and hit the button. Back in her bedroom upstairs, she removed her gray school uniform and skirt, putting them back on the wall hanger.

She put her hands over her chest, feeling for her pulse. The exertion of her bike ride home should have subsided by now, but her heart was still pounding at about ninety beats per minute.

Suguha didn't want to admit that her racing heart had nothing to do with the exercise. She took several deep breaths, but the more she thought about it, the faster it became.

What am I thinking? I'm only showing him the way to Alne. Plus, I already have my big brother to think about. Wait, no, I'm not supposed to think about him! Stupid, stupid, stupid!

Eventually this line of thought drove her to exasperation, so she put on a baggy T-shirt and plopped onto her bed.

The AmuSphere was resting on top of her headboard. She powered it up, put it on, and closed her eyes. One more deep breath, and then the magic spell.

"Link start!"

After the connection phase was finished, she opened her eyes as Leafa, fairy warrior. The vivid surroundings of the Lily of the Valley greeted her.

There was no one in the seat across the table, of course. There was most of an hour to go before they were scheduled to meet up. But she had preparations to make for the journey.

Outside of the tavern, the town of Swilvane was bathed in gorgeous morning light.

A day in ALfheim Online lasted about sixteen hours, perhaps to bring variety to those players who could only log in at a specific time of day. Sometimes it would be the same time in game as it was in the real world, and sometimes—such as now—it was completely off. The time readout in the menu gave both real time and Alfheim time. It was confusing at first, but Suguha liked this system.

She zipped around from store to store and wrapped up her shopping in time to make it back to the tavern. Just as she pushed open the swinging door, a figure in black was materializing at the table in the back.

Kirito blinked a few times after his login and smiled as he recognized Leafa approaching.

"Sweet, that was good timing."

"Nope, I've been here awhile already. I was just doing some errands first."

"Oh, I see. I suppose I need to get outfitted, too, huh."

"Don't worry about the usable items; I got us a healthy supply. Oh, but—" She cast a glance at Kirito's starter equipment. "We might want to buy you some better gear."

"Yeah, I'd love to get something better. This sword is not going to cut it…"

"Do you have money? I can lend you some if you need it."

"Umm…"

Kirito swung his left hand to open the menu and perused it for a moment. For some reason, he frowned.

"…Is this the money in this game? Yrd?"

"That's it. Got any?"

"Uh, actually, I do. Quite a lot."

"In that case, let's get you some gear."

"Um, okay."

Kirito stood and started examining himself all over, as though suddenly remembering something. Finally, he peered into his shirt pocket.

"Hey, Yui. Time to go."

The little black-haired pixie popped her sleepy face out of the pocket and yawned widely.

Once Kirito had outfitted himself with a proper set of equipment at Leafa's favorite armory, the town was fully drenched in the light of the morning sun.

It wasn't a fancy set of armor. Just a clothing-style top and bottom with better defensive properties and a long coat. Most of the time was taken up by Kirito's exacting search for the right sword.

Every time the player who ran the store handed him a new long sword, he'd give it a single swing and say, "Heavier." He only finally gave in and compromised on a greatsword nearly his own height in length. It was immensely imposing and dark, probably meant for the giant players more commonly found in the gnome and imp factions.

Damage in ALO was calculated only from the weapon's attack power and the speed of the swing. This gave an advantage to sylphs and cait siths, who had the highest agility of all the races. So as a balancing measure, muscular players were given better control over the massive weapons with the highest damage stats.

Even a sylph could fight with a hammer or ax with enough work on his skills, but his strength—a fixed, hidden statistic—would be too low to make those weapons worth using in battle. The spriggans were among the more versatile of the in-game races, but Kirito's body type was clearly built for speed, not strength.

"Can you actually swing that thing?" Leafa asked, exasperated.

Kirito nodded coolly. "No problem."

She had no choice but to take his word for it. He paid the shopkeeper's price and hoisted the massive blade onto his back. The tip of the scabbard nearly dragged along the ground.

He's like a child playing at being a warrior, Leafa thought, stifling a laugh.

"Well, I think we're ready to leave! Put 'er there, partner!" She held out her right hand, and Kirito shyly returned the gesture.

"Nice working with you."

The pixie zipped out of his pocket and flew over to smack both of their hands in celebration as she spoke.

"We can do it! To the World Tree!"

Massive sword on his back and diminutive pixie on his shoulder, Kirito followed alongside Leafa for several minutes, until she spotted the shining, jade-green tower ahead.

It was the Tower of Wind, the symbol of the sylph homeland. No matter how many times Leafa saw it, she never failed to marvel at its beauty. When she gave Kirito a sidelong glance, however, the spriggan was distastefully eyeing the tower wall he'd been so intimate with the day before. She jabbed him with an elbow, holding back her laughter.

"Want a lesson on braking before we get flying again?"

"...Not necessary. I'm sticking to safe flying from now on," he answered brusquely. "What's up with the tower? Are we doing something here?"

"You'll want to use these towers for long-distance flight. The extra altitude makes all the difference."

"Aha, I see, " he nodded. Leafa gave him a push on the back.

"Let's get going! We'll want to be out of the forest by nightfall."

"Well, I don't know the terrain at all, so show me the way."

"You're in good hands!" She tapped her chest and turned to look beyond the tower.

The majestic silhouette of the sylph lord's mansion was clear against the morning sun. The owner of the mansion was a female player named Sakuya, someone Leafa had known throughout her time playing. She thought briefly of stopping by to give her regards before leaving, but the flag bearing the sylph crest was nowhere to be seen on the flagpole sprouting from the center of the building's roof. It was an indication of the rare occurrence when the master was not home for the day.

"What's up?" Kirito asked quizzically, but Leafa shook her head. She made a mental note to send a message to Sakuya later, then turned back to the business at hand and strode through the door of the tower.

The ground floor of the structure was a wide, circular lobby with a variety of shops lining the wall. In the center of the lobby were two elevators that presumably ran on magic, sucking in and spitting out players at regular intervals. It was early morning in Alfheim but evening in the real world, so the milling population was starting to grow as more players logged in.

She pulled Kirito by the arm toward the elevator on the right. It had just descended to their level when several figures suddenly moved into place to block their path. Just before she collided with them, Leafa spread her wings to come to a stop.

"Hey, watch it!" she snapped instinctively, then recognized the tall man who had stepped in her way.

He was far above the average sylph height, with rough but masculine features. He was either very lucky or very rich to have obtained looks like those. His body was clad in thick silver armor, and a large broadsword hung from his waist. There was a wide silver band around his forehead, and flowing, dark green locks extended down to his shoulders.

The man's name was Sigurd. He was a frontline fighter in the party Leafa had been working with for the past few weeks. She noticed that the others he was standing with were those very same party members. She looked around to see if Recon was among them, but there was no sign of his characteristic golden-green hair.

Sigurd was a power player, a constant rival with Leafa for the title of the strongest sylph. And unlike Leafa, who avoided the struggles for control over the sylph populace, he willingly took part in the game's politics. The current sylph lord—elected by popular vote monthly, with the power to set taxes and determine their use—was Sakuya, but Sigurd was a visible figure as her right-hand man, an ultra-active player in the community.

His vast playtime earned him skill numbers and equipment that Leafa could never hope to match. Whenever they dueled, it was always a protracted, painful affair in which Leafa tried to use her superb athleticism to overcome his stalwart defense. As a hunting partner, he was a reliable force, but his pushy, bossy personality was distasteful to Leafa, who wanted to be free to pursue her own whims. The present arrangement was certainly a lucrative one for her, but she'd been thinking it was about time to part ways.

Fittingly, the smile on Sigurd's face as he loomed imposingly over her was tilted into his most imperious and haughty sneer. This was not going to be fun, she knew.

"Hello, Sigurd," she grinned, but he did not return the pleasantry. Instead, he launched into his business with a growl.

"Are you leaving the party, Leafa?"

He was clearly in a foul mood, and she briefly thought of reassuring him that it was only going to be a brief trip to Alne and back. But the weight of all her concerns was too much, and Leafa found the simpler answer was to nod and own it.

"Yeah... I suppose. I've made plenty of money doing this, so I'm going to take it easy for a bit."

"How very selfish. And you don't think that will harm the other members?"

"Wha—? Selfish...?!"

That set her off. At the dueling tournament two months ago, after Leafa had defeated Sigurd in a close contest, he approached her later to admit that he was scouting her for his party. She'd thought she made it clear to him that she had conditions: She would only participate in the party's activities when convenient for her, and she could leave whenever she wanted. It was supposed to be a no-strings-attached arrangement.

Sigurd raised his bushy eyebrows and continued, "You're already well known as a member of my party. If you leave us without a good reason and join another party, it shames us and ruins our good name."

"..."

Leafa was speechless. The arrogance of such a claim... But deep down, a part of her had known this moment was coming.

After she'd been in Sigurd's party for a while, Recon—who'd also been admitted as her sidekick of sorts—had given her a serious warning.

He'd said it was a bad idea to get in too deep with this group. He suspected that Sigurd hadn't scouted Leafa for her battle ability but for her intangible marketing value for his brand. Not only that, but by recruiting the warrior who'd beaten him as a teammate—no, a subordinate—he protected himself against any loss of prestige from that defeat.

Leafa had tried to laugh off the suggestion, but Recon persisted. In a hard-core skill-oriented MMO like ALO, female players were a rarity, which made their in-game value based more on their pop-star status than their abilities. According to Recon, a girl as talented and, more importantly, *attractive* as Leafa was rarer than a legendary weapon, making her a desired piece of eye candy, not to mention the target of less savory desires, which of course *he* did not share, being a true friend who only wanted a real, platonic relationship and none of those other benefits, you can be assured.

Leafa had given him a solid blow to the liver with all of her weight to stop him from elaborating on that particular train of thought. Once that was taken care of, she considered his point. First of all, she didn't get the sense that she was inspiring any kind of celebrity treatment. On top of that, there were enough things to keep track of in an MMORPG that she didn't feel like complicating matters further. She'd decided to keep taking part in Sigurd's group, and there hadn't been any major problems... until now.

Faced with a furious Sigurd, Leafa felt the heavy, clinging web of hassles descending upon her. The only thing she wanted from ALO was the feeling of flight, of escape from pressure. To cast aside her troubles and fly as far as she desired. Nothing more.

But it seemed that was a naiveté born of ignorance. Perhaps it was just a fantasy of hers, that this virtual world where everyone had wings would be enough to help her forget the gravity of real life.

She thought back to the older boy from the kendo dojo who had picked on her in elementary school. He'd been invincible since joining the dojo, until he could no longer beat Suguha—younger and, even worse, a girl. So he'd gathered his friends to play a mean prank on her on the way home. That boy's mouth had been arched in the same arrogant smile that Sigurd wore now.

So this place is just the same…

Leafa cast her head down, devastated by frustration and disappointment. Suddenly, Kirito, who had silently melted like a shadow behind her, spoke up.

"Companions aren't items."

"Huh…?"

Leafa spun around, wide-eyed. In the moment, she didn't understand what he meant. Sigurd growled in surprise.

"What did you say?"

Kirito stepped forward between Leafa and Sigurd, staring down the imposing figure who stood a full head taller than him. "Your fellow players aren't swords or pieces of armor. You can't just lock them down in equipment slots."

"H-how dare you—!" Sigurd's face went an instant red at Kirito's direct challenge. He swiped his long cape back and placed a threatening hand on his sword hilt.

"Miserable, trash-digging spriggan! Quit wasting your time with scum like him, Leafa! He's likely just another renegade exiled from his home territory!"

His insult was so furious that he seemed on the verge of drawing his blade at any moment. But Leafa had lost her composure and shouted back.

"Watch your mouth! I'll have you know Kirito is my new partner!"

"What…?" A blue vein was pulsing on Sigurd's forehead as he grunted in shock. "Leafa… are you abandoning our territory?"

Those words caused her eyes to go wide.

Players in ALO were widely separated into two groups, based on their play style.

One of those groups was made of people like Leafa and Sigurd, who used their race's territory as a home base, worked with others of their own kind, and paid yrd tithes to their race's government to increase the group's power within the game. The other kind of player left the territory for neutral ground and worked with parties of mixed races. The former looked down on the latter for being aimless, calling them renegades—either for leaving home of their own accord or being exiled by the lord of the territory.

Leafa felt little affiliation to the general collective of sylphs; she stuck around because she liked Swilvane and didn't want the disruption of pulling up her roots and leaving. But Sigurd's accusations accelerated her desire to be free of this nonsense, forcing her to confront her inner conflict.

"Yes…that's right. I'm leaving," she said simply.

Sigurd's lips twisted to expose his clenched teeth, and he drew his broadsword. He glared at Kirito with eyes aflame.

"I had no intention of bothering myself with the buzzing of insignificant flies, but your brazen attempt at thievery cannot be overlooked. Surely you are prepared for the possibility of being cut down where you stand in another race's territory…"

Kirito answered Sigurd's theatrical menace with only a shrug of his shoulders. Leafa nearly rolled her eyes at his sheer nerve, but she put her hand on her katana anyway, just in case she had to attack Sigurd. The air was tense.

Suddenly, one of Sigurd's fellows piped up quietly from behind him.

"Now's not a good time, Sig. You can't just kill an unresisting player in public like this…"

Perhaps sensing that trouble was about to erupt, a ring of observers had formed around them. Proper duels or accusations of spying aside, Kirito was nothing more than a simple tourist, and an act of open aggression from Sigurd would not reflect well on him.

Sigurd glared at Kirito, teeth gnashing, but reluctantly returned his sword to its sheath.

"Make sure you stay well out of sight out there," he shot at Kirito, before turning his attention to Leafa. "If you betray me now, you'll rue your choice later."

"Much better than regretting my choice to stay."

"Then you ought to practice begging on your hands and knees

for when you want to come back to the fold," Sigurd menaced, then spun around and headed for the tower's exit. His two party members looked at Leafa as though they wanted to say something, but ultimately they gave up and ran after Sigurd.

Only when they were out of sight did Leafa let out a heavy sigh. "I'm sorry for getting you involved in that…"

"No, I shouldn't have fanned the flames the way I did. Are you sure about this, though? You're really leaving your territory?"

"Uhh…"

Leafa struggled to find something to say at first, then pushed Kirito on the back without any elaboration. They made their way through the circle of observers and hopped onto the elevator. She hit the button for the top floor, and the large stone circle that served as the elevator platform glowed green and shot up through the clear glass tube.

Less than a minute later, the elevator came to a stop, and the glass wall opened without a sound, letting in the white morning sun and a pleasant breeze.

Leafa quickly paced out onto the observation deck on the tower's top level. She'd been to this landing countless times, but the open panorama in all directions never failed to make her heart spring to life.

The sylph territory was in the southwest region of Aincrad. To the west was a stretch of plains that abruptly met the sea, an infinite expanse of blue water. To the east was an endless forest bordered by the purple haze of a mountain range. Beyond them, looming even larger and virtually the same shade as the sky above, was one enormous shadow—the World Tree.

"Wow…what a view," Kirito marveled, squinting as he scanned the horizon. "The sky's so close, I feel like I could reach out and grab it…"

He stared out at the blue with eyes full of longing. Leafa extended her hand into the air and said, "Right? When you gaze out at this sky, it makes everything else seem insignificant in comparison."

"..."

Kirito gave her a concerned look. She smiled back to reassure him. "It's for the best, really. I was looking for the chance to leave anyway. I was just too afraid to make the plunge on my own..."

"I see. But now you really burned your bridges on the way out..."

"After his reaction, I doubt there was any peaceful way to leave the party. I wonder," she started to mumble, mostly to herself. "Why does everything have to come down to control-or-be-controlled? I mean, we have these wonderful wings..."

It wasn't Kirito who answered her but the pixie named Yui, whose face was propped up on his wide jacket collar. "Humans are very complicated things."

She spun into the air with a jingle and landed on Kirito's other shoulder, crossing her arms and muttering, "I do not understand the nature of humanity to make the search for the hearts of others such a complicated process."

Leafa stared at Yui, briefly forgetting that she was only a program.

"The search for...?"

"I understand that the root cause of much human behavior is the desire to interact with the hearts of other people. This is the foundation of my understanding. In my case..." Yui suddenly put a hand on Kirito's cheek and gave him a dainty kiss. "I do this. It is a very simple and clear way to demonstrate that desire."

Leafa's eyes went wide with surprise, but Kirito laughed uneasily and flicked Yui's head.

"The human world is a bit more complex than that. If everyone tried it, they'd cross the harassment code and get banned."

"It's a matter of sequence and style, right?"

"Please don't pick up nonsense like that, Yui."

Leafa finally found her voice and butted into the conversation. "Th-that's quite a remarkable AI. Are all private pixies like her?"

"No, she's especially weird," Kirito remarked, picking up Yui by the lapel and depositing her back into his shirt pocket.

"I…see. Searching for the hearts of others, huh?" she repeated, then stretched her back out.

Leafa's personal desire was to fly as far as she could across this world. Did this mean that underneath that exterior, she simply needed to connect with another person? Kazuto's face suddenly flashed through her head, and she felt her heart leap within her chest.

Perhaps what she really wanted…was to use these fairy wings to fly over all those obstacles in real life, until she finally reached Kazuto's heart.

"Yeah, right…"

I'm overthinking, she told herself. *I just want to fly. That's all.*

"Hmm? You say something?"

"N-nothing…Let's get going, shall we?"

She cast a smile toward Kirito and looked up into the sky. The clouds that had been glowing gold during the sunrise had dissipated by now, leaving only unbroken blue. It was going to be a lovely day.

There was a monument on the platform called a Locator Stone that Leafa instructed Kirito to use—it would bookmark his location so that he could return later. Once that was done, she stretched and beat her four wings.

"All ready?"

"Yeah."

Kirito checked with the pixie in his pocket to confirm she was ready as well, but before they could start flying…

"Leafa!"

A figure behind them was practically falling out of the elevator, he was in such a rush. Leafa lowered herself back onto the platform.

"Oh…Recon."

"Th-this isn't right! You could have told me before you left."

"Sorry, Recon! I forgot."

He tried to pull himself together, and when he looked up at her, it was with a serious expression on his face.

"I heard…you're leaving the party?"

"Half out of impulse, really. What are you going to do now?"

"Isn't that obvious? My sword exists only for you, Leafa…"

"Ugh, I didn't ask for that."

Recon slumped his shoulders again, but this wasn't enough to stop him.

"Well, I'd like to go with you, of course…but there's something weighing on my mind."

"…What's that?"

"I'm not certain of it yet…but I need to be sure. So I'm going to stay in Sigurd's party for a bit longer. Kirito?" Now he fixed Kirito with his most serious gaze. "She has a bad habit of jumping into trouble. So watch out."

"Um, yeah…got it," Kirito nodded, seemingly entertained.

"And just so you know, she's my— Gack!" Leafa's boot landing on the bridge of his foot, hard, cut him short.

"Enough out of you! I'll be in neutral for a good while, so send me a message if anything happens!" she chattered hastily, then spread her wings and took to the air. Leafa waved down at Recon, who was looking up unhappily. "And make sure to keep practicing your Voluntary Flight, even while I'm gone. Also, stay away from salamander territory! 'Bye!"

"S-stay safe, Leafa! I'll catch up to you soon!" he wailed, tears in his eyes. *I'm going to see you at school tomorrow, you dip,* Leafa thought, but she was surprised to find a touch of emotion at the parting, and she turned away before it could develop into anything. She set her sights to the northeast and spread her wings for a glide.

Kirito pulled up to her side within moments, clearly struggling to hide a grin.

"Is he a real-life friend of yours?"

"…You could say that."

"Ohh?"

"…What? Is that interesting to you?"

"Just thinking that it's…nice."

Yui spoke up from Kirito's pocket. "I can understand his emotions. He likes you, Leafa. What do you think of that?"

"I-I don't care!!" she shouted, increasing her speed to hide her embarrassment. She was used to Recon's open attitude about his feelings, but she felt strangely self-conscious when he did it with Kirito around.

In quick order, they had left the town and were surrounded by the green of the forest. Leafa flipped around onto her back and looked at the shrinking jade city.

Something like wistful longing pricked her heart when she thought of leaving Swilvane, her in-game home for the past year, but that pain was washed away by the excitement of a journey to new, unfamiliar surroundings. She said a silent good-bye and turned back over.

"Let's hurry! We can make it to that lake in a single flight!"

She pointed at the sparkling water far in the distance and beat her wings.

—◊◊◊—

Asuna simply closed her eyes and shut out the sensation of the clinging, clammy fingertip sliding along the underside of her arm.

They were on the enormous bed in the middle of the birdcage. Oberon was stretched out on his side, long green toga in a disheveled state around his body as he held Asuna's hand and rubbed her skin. His handsome face was even creepier and more loathsome than usual—he was clearly enjoying toying with her, knowing she would be at his mercy if he chose to take her.

When Oberon had entered the cage and sprawled out on the bed, she initially resisted his command to join him. When he started fiddling with her arm, she nearly punched his lights out.

The only reason she swallowed her disgust and obeyed him was the knowledge of his mercurial temper: She was afraid of him stealing what little freedom she still possessed. In fact, it was almost as though he was *waiting* for her to resist. He would wait until he'd drunk his fill of her displeasure, then use his system privileges to have his way with her. At least for the moment, she was free to walk around the inside of the cage. She had to keep it that way...if she wanted any chance of escape.

But there were limits to what she could stand. If he touched her body, she would put her right fist smack in the middle of his face. Until then, she remained as still as stone, until Oberon gave up on getting any reaction from stroking her arm. He let go and sat up.

"Why do you have to be so headstrong?" he pouted. That voice was the one thing about Oberon that perfectly matched her memory of Sugou, and it made her sick all over again. "It's not even your real body. There's no lasting harm. Isn't it boring spending all your time in here? Haven't you ever thought about just enjoying it?"

"You don't understand. Real or virtual makes no difference. At least to me."

"Why? Because it will ruin the purity of your heart?" He chuckled deep in his throat. "Well, I'm certainly not letting you out of here until I've solidified my position a bit more. I think it would be smarter of you to learn how to enjoy it while you can. The system here is really quite deep in its simulation, didn't you know?"

"I have no interest in that. Besides, I'm not going to be in here forever. I have faith that he'll come for me."

"Oh? Who will? Kirito the Hero, you mean?"

Asuna's body trembled unconsciously at the name. Oberon's leer widened as he sat up straighter. He began speaking faster now, satisfied that he'd finally found her button and knew how to push it.

"What was his actual name...? Kirigaya? I met him the other day. On the other side."

"...!!"

The moment she heard that, Asuna lifted her head and looked straight at him.

"I tell you, I couldn't believe my eyes when I saw that the hero who beat SAO was that scrawny little boy! Or is that just what all hard-core gamers look like?" He egged her on, delight plastered over his face. "Where do you suppose I saw him? In your hospital room, right next to your body. I wish you could have seen his face when I told him I was going to marry you next month, as you lay in your bed next to us! I've seen dogs with their favorite bones taken away who looked less pitiful than he did. I nearly burst out laughing!"

His body shook and gyrated with mirth as he let out odd little gasping giggles.

"So you actually believe that little kid's going to come save you! I'd bet good money that he doesn't have the guts to even put a NerveGear on his head ever again! To say nothing of him ever actually finding you here. Hey, that reminds me, I still need to send him a wedding invitation. I'm sure he'll be there—he'll want to see you in your wedding dress. I mean, we have to give our precious hero *something* to hang on to, don't we?"

Asuna lowered her head once more, turned her back on Oberon, and faced the large mirror that hung from the bed's canopy frame. The strength drained from her shoulders, and she squeezed the cushions tight.

"Alas, the security cameras were off, so I didn't get a recording of his utter disappointment. I could have brought you a video souvenir. Maybe I'll try that next time. But for now, I'm afraid I must take my leave, Titania. Do try to fight the loneliness until I visit you in two days' time."

With a final chuckle, Oberon turned over and walked to the door, his toga swaying.

Asuna watched him grow smaller in the mirror as she made a point of sobbing. Inwardly, she screamed a silent exultation.

Kirito... Kirito is alive!

That had been her greatest concern since she'd been taken prisoner in this new world. The possibility that she'd been sent somewhere else while Kirito was simply gone forever had slowly but steadily dripped its toxins over her heart, even as she told herself it wasn't true.

But without realizing it, Oberon had just wiped that worry clean from her mind.

For such a smart man, he could be truly stupid—he'd always been that way. He just couldn't resist the urge to talk down to others. He played coy in front of Asuna's parents, but Asuna and her brother had been witness to Sugou's haughty insults on many occasions.

This was a perfect example. If he really wanted to break Asuna's will, he shouldn't have run his mouth about Kirito. He should have told her he was dead.

Kirito was alive. He was back in the real world.

She repeated the words over and over to herself, savoring them. Each time she did, the flame inside her heart grew hotter and brighter.

If he was alive, he wouldn't turn a blind eye to what was happening. He would find this game and come for her. That meant she couldn't just play the helpless prisoner. She had to do whatever she could to escape.

She faced the mirror and pretended to be grief stricken. In its reflection, she could see Oberon turn around at the door and glance at her to check on what she was doing.

Next to the door was a small metallic plate with twelve tiny buttons. There was a passcode that he typed in each time to open and close the door.

It seemed rather unnecessary to Asuna. Why not simply set the properties of the cage such that only an admin could open the door? But Oberon seemed to have his own exacting standards for this place, and he did not want to betray the illusion of the game. In here, he was the king of the fairies, the tyrant who ruled his queen with an iron fist.

Another flaw stemming from his foolish arrogance.

Oberon lifted a hand to fiddle with the pad. He was far enough away from Asuna that the game's distance filter blurred the details of which buttons he pressed. He knew that she couldn't tell from there, and thus he thought his cage to be inescapable.

That much was correct—if she were looking directly at Oberon.

But he didn't have much experience with the actual details of the virtual world that the NerveGear created. There were many things he didn't know yet. Such as, for example, the fact that mirrors were not treated as optical effects.

Asuna was pretending to cry while squinting directly into the mirror at close range. Oberon was crystal clear. A real mirror would not make a distant object any clearer, no matter how close you sat, but the game treated the surface of the mirror as a pristine reflection. The normal distance obfuscation the game's engine used was not applied to the reflection. As a result, she could see perfectly, down to the movements of his fingertips.

She'd had this idea quite a long time ago. But until today, there'd been no natural way for her to be next to the mirror when he was at the door. She couldn't miss this opportunity.

8...11...3...2...9.

She repeated the buttons that pale finger touched, over and over. The door opened, Oberon passed through it, and it shut again with a heavy *clank*. Through the bars, she saw the fairy king walk along the branch, his black-and-emerald wings waving, until he passed out of sight.

Asuna patiently waited and waited for the metal bar pattern painted on the floor of the birdcage by the light of the sun to change.

She had not gained much information to this point.

This was another VRMMO much like Sword Art Online titled ALfheim Online, and shockingly enough, it was actually in business and taking new users. Oberon (Sugou) was using the ALO server to imprison the minds of about three hundred former SAO players, and he was planning to use them for illegal brain experiments. That was all.

When she'd asked why he would risk the danger of running illegal experiments inside a well-known video game, he'd simply snorted at her. "Please. Do you have any idea how much it costs to run a system like this? Millions and millions of yen for a single server! But this setup will allow me to further my research *and* let the company make money at the same time. Two birds with one stone!"

So it came down to profit. This worked in Asuna's favor, however. There would be no way out of a completely closed environment, but since this game was connected to people out in the real world, she would have a chance.

She'd managed to sneak enough information out of Oberon to know that days passed here faster than in the real world. That meant it would be difficult to determine the real time outside, but once again, it was Oberon himself who provided her with the means to solve the problem.

She knew that he came to her once every other day, after work, using a company terminal. He valued his regular schedule and was punctual to a fault, so she was confident that his visits were at the same time each day. That meant the smartest time to strike was after he left for home and went to sleep.

He wouldn't have orchestrated this conspiracy all on his own, of course. But it was clearly a criminal act. She didn't think that the entire maintenance team of ALO was involved. It would only be a few...and if they all reported to Nobuyuki Sugou directly, they couldn't possibly monitor ALO all night long. No office employee could work full-night shifts every day of the week.

If she could just escape the birdcage when they weren't watching, find her way to a system console somehow, and log out... And if that weren't possible, there must be some way to send a message to the outside. She rolled over onto her stomach, face buried in the pillow, and simply waited for time to pass.

———

Leafa watched Kirito fight with half wonder, half disbelief.

They were in the air over the Ancient Forest in the northeast stretch of sylph territory, just before the woods gave way to rolling plains. Swilvane was far in the rearview mirror, the jade tower well out of view by now.

Because they were deep in the neutral territory between safe havens, the monsters were of a high level. Kirito was fighting three Evil Glancers, giant one-eyed winged lizards. The beasts were each as strong as the boss of the starter dungeon in the sylph homeland.

They were quite powerful, naturally, but the real menace they posed was in their Evil Eye ability, a magical curse attack that temporarily reduced the victim's stats. Leafa kept her distance to provide backup, casting a curse-nullification spell every time Kirito got hit, but she was beginning to wonder if that was even necessary.

Kirito swung his mammoth sword with berserk abandon— the words *defense* and *evasion* did not exist in his dictionary. He devastated the lizards with his tremendous swings, and he didn't seem to even register their long-distance tail attacks. The maelstrom of his charges often enveloped multiple lizards in a single blow. Most frightening of all was the sheer damage every hit inflicted. There had been five Evil Glancers to start with, and in no time at all, they were down to one, which turned tail and fled for the trees when it fell below 20 percent HP, shrieking piteously. Leafa held out her hand and fired a long-range homing vacuum spell. Four or five glowing green boomerang-shaped blades converged on the lizard's body, shearing away scales. The blue reptile burst into a cloud of polygonal shards, and their fifth battle of the day was over just barely after it had begun.

Kirito loudly sheathed his blade and bobbed through the air over to Leafa, who gave him a brief salute.

"Nice work."

"Thanks for the backup."

They slapped palms and smiled.

"You know what? You fight like a crazy person," Leafa remarked. Kirito scratched his head.

"Y-you think so?"

"Normally you're supposed to prioritize evasion and dart around, but you're just hit, hit, and hit."

"Hey, it finished the battle quicker, right?"

"That might work against a group of the same monster. But if you go up against close- and long-range foes at once, or a party of other players, they'll snipe at you with magic."

"Can't you avoid magic?"

"There are different kinds of spells. The really heavy blasts that fire in a straight line can be dodged if you see them coming, but not the good homing or area-of-effect spells. If you run across a mage using those spells, you have to keep moving at top speed and try to time it so you don't get caught."

"Well, there was no magic in the last game I played...I've got a lot of new stuff to learn, I guess." He scratched his head like a child being faced with a particularly tough test question.

"I'm sure you'll pick it up in no time. You've got very good eyes. Do you play sports or something?"

"Nope, not at all."

"Oh...well, whatever. Let's keep going."

"Yeah."

They nodded and flapped their wings. Beyond the edge of the forest, the golden-green of the plains beckoned them, reflecting the light of the sun in its descent.

There were no more monsters after that. They emerged from the Ancient Forest and headed into a rocky hillscape. The mountains were designed so that they loomed well above the flight altitude limit, so the pair had to land in a corner of the plain that served as the foot of the range.

Leafa skidded to a landing, boots sliding on the grass, her arms outstretched. Oddly enough, even though it wasn't a real part of her body, she couldn't shake the sensation that the base of her wings was tired. A few seconds later, Kirito landed and used the opportunity to stretch out his back.

"Heh, tired?"

"Nope, not a bit!"

"Good to hear…but as a matter of fact, we're done flying for a while."

Kirito's eyebrows rose at Leafa's words. "Oh? Why?"

"See these mountains?" She pointed at the series of peaks capped in white, looming over the plains. "They're taller than the altitude limit for flying, so you have to go through a cave to get past them. It's the trickiest part of the journey from sylph lands to Alne—or so I hear; I've never been past this point."

"All right, then. Is the cave long?"

"Very. There's a neutral mining town inside where you can rest, though. How are you for time, Kirito?"

He waved his left hand to check the clock in his menu and nodded.

"Seven o'clock outside. I'm fine for now."

"Let's keep going, then. Wanna rotate out here?"

"Rotate…out?"

"It means taking turns logging out to rest. This is neutral territory, so you can't just log out immediately. Instead, by taking turns, the person online can protect the other's empty avatar."

"Ah, got it. You can go first, Leafa."

"All right, see you in twenty minutes, then!"

She opened her window and hit the log-out button. Next came a confirmation warning, which she accepted, and the scenery around her flowed far, far away, until it became a single point and disappeared.

Suguha popped awake on her bed and leaped up, almost too impatient to remove her AmuSphere. She left the room and snuck down the stairs. Midori's magazine deadline was coming up, so she was still at work, and Kazuto was in his room. It was silent downstairs.

She opened the refrigerator and pulled out two bagels, sliced ham, mustard, and a few vegetables. She sliced the bagels quickly, spread a thin layer of mustard, and topped it with the ham and veggies. Each bagel sandwich went on its own plate. She then poured some milk into a pan and set it on the induction stove before heading back up the stairs.

"Big brother, what do you want for dinner?"

There was no response. She shrugged and returned to the kitchen, assuming he was asleep. The gently steaming milk went into a big mug, which she carried to the living room table with the plates of food. After a brief grace, she ate her simple dinner in barely ninety seconds and dumped the dish into the sink before rushing to the bathroom. Even in the virtual world, the rigors of battle made her sweat, so she always needed to clean up and change clothes after a long dive.

She stripped off her clothes at light speed and leaped into the shower room, spraying the hot water directly on her head.

Midori would scold Suguha if she let the VRMMO take attention away from meals or bathing, so she made sure to schedule any group activities before the evening. But this case was different. This journey with Kirito would last all of tomorrow, if not the day after. Normally, Suguha was not a big fan of long-term party play, and she balked at multiday activities, but this was different somehow. In fact…

I'm excited about it, she told herself, shower water running over her closed eyelids.

When she opened her eyes, they stared back at her in the mirror directly in front of her. In those black pupils she saw eagerness and just a bit of apprehension.

Suguha's stature was far from large for a kendo athlete, but compared to Leafa the sylph, she was rather big-boned. When she moved her shoulders, stomach, or thighs, the muscles rose to the surface of the skin. She thought her breasts had grown quite a bit recently, too.

She couldn't help but feel that the inescapable *reality* of that body reflected her own inner conflict, so Suguha shut her eyes tight again.

Well, it's not like I'm in love with him. I'm excited about the new world I'm about to venture into, not the person it happens to be with. That's all.

Those words weren't just something she tried to tell herself. They were the honest truth.

Looking back, every day used to be that way.

The stronger she grew, the wider her range of activities. Just flying through the sky over unfamiliar territory was a thrill. But as she became one of the strongest sylphs in the game, along with her knowledge came hassles. In time, she felt she was just going through the motions. The obligation to fight for her race became an invisible chain shackled to her wings.

The term *renegade*, used to refer to those who abandoned their homeland, was an English word that could also mean *heretic*. People who gave up on the duty placed on their shoulders and were exiled in response…She'd thought of them as simple traitors, but now she wondered if those renegades were actually just guilty of nothing more than a sense of pride.

Her mind wandered over this topic while her hands kept busy, scrubbing her hair and body and washing off the suds. She grabbed a dry towel off the wall and fiddled with the wall panel next to it. A slit on the ceiling started blustering hot air down on her. Once her hair was mostly dry, she wrapped herself in the large towel and ran back into the living room. She checked the clock: Seventeen of the allotted twenty minutes had already passed.

Suguha wrapped the other sandwich in plastic and ripped a note off the pad. She scrawled, "Eat this if you get hungry, big brother," and stuck it under the plate.

She flew up the stairs and slipped into a fresh outfit, crawling onto her bed and putting on the AmuSphere, still in suspended mode.

The connection test crawled by with agonizing slowness. Through the rainbow ring she went at last, and the gentle breeze of the plains tickled Leafa's nose.

* * *

"Thanks for waiting! Any monsters?" Leafa asked, rising from the one-legged crouch that the game always started in. Kirito was lying on the grass nearby, and he removed a green straw-like object from his mouth to speak.

"Nope, all quiet here."

"What's that?"

"I bought a bunch of them at a general store before we left. The NPC said they were a specialty unique to Swilvane."

"I've never heard of that."

Kirito tossed the pipe to her. She caught it and put it in her mouth, hoping a blank face would hide her fluster. The drag of air she took tasted of sweet peppermint.

"Now it's my turn to log out. Thanks for standing guard."

"Yep, see you soon."

When he logged out, his body automatically assumed the standby crouch. Leafa sat down next to him and gazed up at the sky, puffing on the minty pipe, until she was startled by the tiny fairy who wriggled her way out of the shirt pocket of Kirito's still form.

"*Pwaa!* Y-you can move without your master?"

Yui nodded, hands on her little waist, as though this was obvious to anyone.

"Of course—I'm me. And he's not my master; he's my papa."

"Speaking of which, why do you call him Papa? Is that what he set your relationship to be?"

"...Papa saved me. He said I was his child. Which makes him my papa."

"I...see..." Leafa lied. "Do you love your papa?"

She intended it as an innocent question, but Yui fixed her with a deadly serious gaze.

"Leafa...what does love mean?"

"Um, it means..." She trailed off and had to stop and think. "You want to be with someone at all times. Your heart races when you're around them...Stuff like that, I guess."

Kazuto's smile crossed her mind—and for some reason, it overlapped with the face of the avatar kneeling next to her, eyes closed. Leafa held her breath. When she realized that the affection for Kazuto she'd kept hidden in her heart for so long might be happening with Kirito as well, she had to shake her head to clear it. Yui was puzzled.

"What's the matter, Leafa?"

"N-n-nothing at all!" she yelped. The next instant—

"What's nothing?"

"Aaah!!"

Leafa literally leaped up into the air when she noticed Kirito had raised his head.

"Well, here I am. Did anything happen?" he nonchalantly asked the panicked Leafa, rising to his feet from the standby position. Still perched on his shoulder, Yui squeaked, "Welcome back, Papa! I was just talking with Leafa about what it means to be in lo—"

"I-I said it was n-nothing!" Leafa hurriedly cut her off. "Y-you're back fast; did you actually eat?" she asked Kirito to change the subject.

"Yep. My family left some food out for me."

"That's nice. Well, let's get going. If we don't get to the mining town before too late, it'll be a pain to log out. C'mon, we're almost to the mouth of the cave!" she jabbered hastily, to Kirito's and Yui's surprise. When they didn't react, she spread her wings and beat them a few times.

"Uh, okay. Yeah, let's go," he agreed, looking hesitant. He spread his wings, but then turned back toward the forest they'd come from.

"...? Is something wrong?"

"I feel like..." He scanned the line of trees with a scowl and a squint. "Someone was watching us...Are there any players nearby, Yui?"

"No, I don't detect any signals," the pixie reported, shaking her head. Rather than being reassured, Kirito looked even more suspicious.

"You *felt* it? Is there a sixth sense inside this game?" Leafa asked. Kirito rubbed his chin.

"It's not worth just writing off…Say that someone's watching you, for example. The system has to scan us, to read the data it gives to him. Some folks say your brain can sense that process happening…in theory."

"If you say so…"

"But if Yui doesn't see anyone, I guess I must have imagined it."

"Well, it could have been a tracer," she muttered. Kirito raised his eyebrows.

"What's that?"

"It's a tracking spell. It takes the form of a tiny familiar and tells the caster the location of the spell's target."

"Sounds convenient. You can't get rid of them?"

"If you can spot the tracer, sure—but the higher the caster's magic skill, the farther distance the spell will work from the target. In the wide-open outdoors like this, it would be basically impossible to stop."

"I see…Well, it might have been my mind playing tricks on me. Let's keep going."

"Okay."

They took flight. The white mountain range loomed overhead, as sheer as cliffs, with a yawning black cave mouth smack in the center. Leafa beat her wings, accelerating toward the evil-looking cave, which seemed to be emitting an ominous chill.

After a few minutes, the group was at the aperture in the rock.

Right in the center of the nearly vertical mountain face was a square hole, as clean as if a giant had chiseled it out. It was three or four times Leafa's height in both directions. Only up close did it become apparent that the sides of the cave were decorated with eerie carvings of monsters. Directly overhead, a much larger demon head menaced all who entered.

"Does this cave have a name?" Kirito asked.

"I think it's called the Lugru Corridor—Lugru being the name of the city down here."

"Ahh. This really reminds me of an old fantasy movie..." He grinned.

Leafa looked at him sidelong. She bet he was talking about that really famous trilogy, based on an even older set of books. Kazuto had the complete collector's edition box set, and she'd snuck it out of his room once to watch the series.

"I know the one. They go through the mountains and into an old underground mine, where a giant demon of fire attacks them, right? Well, you won't find any demons here."

"That's a shame."

"There are orcs, however. If you're that eager for them, I can let you handle the fighting." Leafa turned her head and started marching into the cave.

It was chilly inside the passage, and the light from the outside did not penetrate far into its depths. Darkness closed in around them. She was about to raise a hand and cast a light spell when a thought occurred to her.

"Have you been pumping up your magic skills?" she asked Kirito.

"Uhh, if it's the starter magic I got from this race, at least, yeah... Haven't used it much, though."

"Spriggans are good with magic for caves and dungeons and the like. You've got to have a better light spell than my wind magic."

"Do you know what I should use, Yui?" he asked, scratching his head. Yui popped her head out of his pocket and took on her best educator's tone.

"You should at least read the manual, Papa! The light spell is..."

She enunciated the syllables of the spell clearly, one at a time. Kirito repeated them awkwardly with his hand in the air. Soon a pulse of pale light spread from his hand, and when it enveloped Leafa's body, she could see much better than before. Apparently this was not a simple source of light, but a kind of night-vision spell that enhanced their sight in the dark.

"Wow, that's useful! You spriggans aren't half bad after all."

"Hey, that kinda hurts."

"Hee-hee! But you really should memorize the spells you have. Even crappy spriggan magic might actually mean the difference between life and death...once in a blue moon."

"Wow, that hurts even worse!"

They traded jabs as they descended down the twisting passage. In time, the light from the entrance was gone from sight.

"Uhhm...Ahr-dena-r...ray..."

Kirito was poring over the glowing purple game manual, muttering the unfamiliar words of the spell to himself.

"It's not going to work if you stumble over each and every part. Don't try to just mechanically memorize all the sounds of the words. Learn the meaning of all the Words of Power; then it's easy to figure out the spells based on the combinations and their effects."

Instead of inspiring the black swordsman to learn further, this suggestion sent his head slumping with a deep sigh.

"I thought I was playing games to get away from learning foreign vocabulary words..."

"Just so you know, the top-tier spells are made up of about twenty words each."

"Ugh...I think I'll stick with being a pure fighter."

"No complaining! Now start over from the top."

They'd been in the cave for two hours. The ten or so battles against orcs had been a breeze, and they had no fear of getting lost, thanks to the map Leafa bought in Swilvane. According to that map, they were nearly to a bridge that spanned a massive underground reservoir. On the other side of that bridge was the mining city of Lugru.

Lugru was not as large as the mammoth underground fortress that was the capital of gnome territory, but the ores and veins were rich here, and many merchants and crafters gravitated to it. Yet despite that, they ran across no other players on their trip. The cave was not the best hunting ground, and most sylphs would avoid a place where their advantage in flight was of little use. There was enough space to the corridors to fly, but without any sunlight or moonlight to refuel wing power, there was no way to regain the charge.

Most sylphs who wanted to visit Alne for trading or tourist purposes chose the much longer detour north to cait sith territory, thus avoiding the mountains. The cait siths, recognized by their feline ears and tails, were experts in the Taming skill, which allowed them to control monsters and animals. Throughout the year of history in ALO, the cait siths had traded tamed mounts to the sylphs, and they'd been on good terms. The lords of each territory had remained friendly, and some even said there would be an official alliance soon.

Leafa had a number of cait sith friends, and she considered using that route for this trip, but Kirito's obvious haste led her to choose the shorter way. The underground route made her uneasy, but so far, the going had been quick.

But Kirito's reasons for rushing to Alne and the World Tree were still a mystery to her. His aloof demeanor made it difficult to read his mind, but the way he tore through their battles told her much about his haste.

Leafa remembered him saying that he was looking for someone. Trying to track down someone in a game who couldn't be reached in real life wasn't that strange of a story. There was a bulletin board out front of the general store that was always packed with wanted notices looking for specific players. It usually had to do with grudges to settle or romantic entanglements, but those didn't seem likely to apply to Kirito. Searching in Alne made sense—but why the World Tree? It was unconquered territory at this point. They might reach the foot of the tree, but they couldn't made it to the top...

She continued mulling over this mystery as Kirito stumbled over his spell words. Being lost in thought out in neutral territory was a great way to get killed, but Yui alerted them to the presence of nearby monsters with frightful precision, so there was no danger of ambush.

Several minutes later, when they were nearly at the lake, Leafa was snapped out of her haze of thought—not by Yui but by a sound effect very much like the ringing of an old phone.

She looked up with a start and called out to Kirito.

"Ack! I got a message. Sorry, hang on."

"Sure."

She stopped and touched the floating icon just below her chest. A window opened at once and, sadly, Leafa knew exactly who it would be from—her only registered friend in the game was Recon. She scanned the message quickly, expecting it to be something pointless. But...

JUST LIKE WE THOUGHT! BE CAREFUL, S—

It ended abruptly, mid-message.

"What is this?" she muttered. It made no sense. What did he think? What was she supposed to be careful about? And what was that *s* at the end supposed to mean? If he were signing the message, it would have been an *R*. Did he accidentally send the message before he was done, or did he hit the extra letter by mistake?

"S, s, s...sa...shi...su?"

"What's wrong?" Kirito asked. Just as she was about to describe the message, Yui popped her head out of his shirt pocket.

"Papa, I'm detecting something approaching."

"Monsters?" He put a hand on the hilt of the giant sword slung over his back. But Yui waved her head.

"No, players. Many of them...twelve."

"Twelve?!" Leafa was stunned. It was far too many for an ordinary battle party. Perhaps it was a sylph trading caravan on its way to Lugru or Alne.

About once a month, a large trading caravan was arranged to make a trip to the center of the map. But that was always widely advertised for several days before the journey, in order to recruit volunteers. There was no news of the sort on the bulletin board when she checked this morning.

As long as that mysterious party was made of sylphs, there was no need to fear. It seemed highly unlikely that such a large PK gang would be waiting in a lonely place like this. But despite all of that, Leafa felt uneasy.

"I have a bad feeling about this. We ought to hide and let them pass."

"But...where?" Kirito looked around in confusion. They were in the middle of a long, straight corridor. It was spacious, but there were no branches down that they could hide under.

"Just leave that to me." Leafa grinned confidently, grabbing Kirito's arm and pulling him toward a divot in the rock. She snuggled in close to him, trying to avoid feeling self-conscious, and raised a hand for a magic spell.

A swirling vortex of shining green air sprang up from her feet and enveloped both of them. Their vision was colored just a slight shade of green, but it did mean they'd be virtually invisible from the outside. She turned to Kirito next to her and whispered, "Speak as quietly as possible. Make too much noise, and the spell will break."

"Got it. Real handy spell to have."

Kirito scanned the space outside the veil of wind. Yui whispered from his pocket.

"They'll come into view in two minutes."

Leafa and Kirito pressed themselves against the rock wall. After several tense seconds, Leafa heard the sound of approaching footsteps. She thought she heard the scrape of heavy metal armor, which gave her pause.

Kirito stretched out his neck and peered in the direction of the unidentified party.

"What...is that?"

"What is what? I don't see them yet."

"It doesn't look like a player...Is it a monster? It's like a little tiny red bat..."

"?!"

Leafa's breath caught in her throat. She squinted into the darkness—and saw that a small red shadow was indeed fluttering toward them.

"Crap!"

The curse tore its way out of her throat, unbidden. She rolled out of the hiding spot into the middle of the hallway. The concealing spell was broken, and Kirito hurriedly looked up, confused.

"H-hey, what's the big idea?"

"That's a Tracing Searcher—it's a high-level spell! We have to crush it before it finds us!"

She held out both hands in front of her and began chanting. It was a longer list of words than before, and when it finished, countless needles of emerald green fired from her fingertips. They screamed through the air and bore down on the red shadow.

The bat darted nimbly about, avoiding the projectiles for a time, but their number was too great. Several needles eventually brought it to the ground, where it went up in a tiny flame. Satisfied that the job was done, Leafa turned back to Kirito and screamed, "We've got to run for the town, Kirito!"

"Huh? Shouldn't we hide again?"

"The enemy knows we killed their tracer. Once they get up to this spot, they'll unleash a swarm of searchers—we can't hide anymore. Besides, that was a fire familiar, which means the party on our heels are—"

"Salamanders!" he finished. The heavy metallic marching was growing closer. Leafa turned back and caught a glimpse of red light in the darkness.

"Let's go."

They took off running.

Leafa checked her map as they moved, noting that their current path would take them to the large underground lake very soon. The cave tunnel turned into a bridge splitting the lake, and on the other side was the gate to Lugru, the mining city. In such neutral cities, there was no attacking between player factions, so despite their numbers, the enemy could not hurt them there.

But why such a large party of salamanders...?

Leafa bit her lip. The presence of the tracer meant that they'd been tracking her all along. But Yui's search ability had been in full effect since they left Swilvane. They shouldn't have had the chance. The only way they could have done this was if the spell had been cast on them while they were in town.

There were sylphs who could use fire magic, of course. Each fairy race had an affinity for a certain kind of magic—wind magic for sylphs, earth magic for gnomes, and so on—but any player could learn any magic, provided he or she worked hard enough for it.

But that red bat she'd squashed was a high-level spell combining the pursuit abilities of a tracer and the scrying abilities of a searcher. It would be a herculean effort for a non-salamander to learn a fire spell that advanced. Which meant...

"There was a salamander inside Swilvane?" she muttered to herself as they ran. But that was nearly unthinkable. Swilvane was comparatively open to other races, but salamanders were the enemy, and were subject to considerable scrutiny. If the powerful NPC guardians had noticed any, they would have advanced with blades swinging. There were very few ways to evade that kind of protection...

"Hey, the lake!"

Kirito's cry snapped Leafa back to the matter at hand. She looked up to see the rough stone floor turning to cobblestones ahead, followed by a wide aperture and the dull shine of dark blue water.

The stone bridge extended straight over the center of the lake until it reached the looming castle gate of Lugru on the other side, its wall reaching right to the ceiling of the enormous chamber. If they could just get inside the city, they'd have won the game of tag.

Momentarily relieved, she turned to look back again. There was still quite a gap between them and the red light of their pursuers. She redoubled the pace of her run, feeling confident.

The temperature was slightly cooler over the bridge. They raced through air heavy with the smell of water.

"Looks like we're going to make it."

"Don't get sloppy and fall in the water—there's an enormous monster in the lake."

Just as they reached a circular viewing platform in the dead center of the bridge, two points of light shot through the darkness over their heads from behind. It was the signature glint and sound of a magic explosive. No doubt the salamanders had fired them in desperation, but they failed to aim precisely.

They slowed down, preparing to let the bombs fall and then run past them. The lights dropped about thirty feet ahead.

Leafa held her right arm in front of her face, bracing for the blast, but what occurred took her by surprise. There was a heavy, rumbling roar, and a towering rock face shot up from the surface of the bridge ahead, blocking their progress. She scowled and hissed a curse.

"Oh no…"

"What the—?"

Kirito's eyes went wide, but he didn't slow down. He loudly drew the sword from his back and brandished it as he charged the rock wall.

"Hey—Kirito!" She didn't have time to tell him it wouldn't work. He struck the wall with all of his might, and then flew back to land on his rear. There wasn't even a scratch on the brown rock face.

"…It's pointless," she finished, holding her wings wide to skid to a halt next to Kirito. The spriggan glared up at her.

"You could have told me that sooner…"

"Not with how fast you ran ahead. This is an earth-magic barrier; physical attacks won't hurt it. With enough attack spells, we can knock it down, but…"

"We don't have that much time."

They turned around and saw a group of people clad in shining bloodred armor starting out onto the bridge.

"I don't suppose...we could just fly around it. Maybe jump into the water?" Kirito asked, but she shook her head.

"Nope. Like I just said, there's supposed to be an ultra-high-level water dragon in this lake. Jumping in there without help from an undine is suicide."

"Then I guess we just have to fight."

He readied his giant sword again as Leafa nodded, biting her lip. "It's our only option...but it's not a good one. This is a very high-level earth magic spell for a salamander to be using. There must be an expert mage in their ranks."

Thanks to the narrow width of the bridge, it was at least a guarantee that the enemy couldn't surround them. But it was two against twelve, and they couldn't fly in the dungeon. Leafa couldn't even make use of her greatest skill, aerial combat.

It would all come down to how tough each of the enemy fighters was.

We can't really pin our hopes on that, Leafa thought. She drew her long katana and stood next to Kirito. She could make out the enemy force clearly now, clanking heavily as they marched. Three large salamanders stood in front, covered in thicker armor than the group they'd encountered the other day. Each one had a menacing weapon in his left hand and a large metal shield in his right.

Something caught in Leafa's mind. Because of ALO's realistic simulation, handedness in the game was the same as in real life. The likelihood of all three of them being southpaws was low.

But before she could voice her suspicion, Kirito spoke up.

"It's not that I don't trust your skill in battle, but...do you think you could handle the backup this time?"

"Huh?"

"I want you to hang back and focus on healing. It'll make it easier for me to fight."

She looked at the double-edged sword in his hands again. He had a point—it would be very difficult to use such a weapon in a small space while keeping an eye out not to hit his ally. Being a healer wasn't Leafa's style, but she nodded to him and retreated until her back was nearly against the magic wall. They didn't have time to argue over who did what.

Kirito crouched and twisted, pulling the sword as far behind him as it would go. The three lead salamanders bore down with the force of a tsunami. Kirito's small body twisted until she could almost hear it creaking. Leafa could practically see the pent-up energy billowing around him. The distance closed, until—

"*Sey!!*"

With a shout, Kirito stomped his left foot forward and swung his glowing blue sword in a flat arc at the trio of crimson warriors. The air screamed as it was split, and the bridge shook with his force. It was the most powerful blow Leafa had seen Kirito unleash yet. However...

"Huh?!"

She looked on in shock. The three salamanders didn't raise their weapons. Instead, they crowded close together, raising their heavy shields to form a protective barrier.

There was a deafening *clang* as Kirito's sword hit the line of shields. The shock turned the air electric, and waves rippled out along the lake surface. But the soldiers had stood firm against his attack and only been pushed back inches.

Leafa hurriedly checked their HP. The warriors had each lost more than 10 percent. But soon the sound of spells echoed forth from behind them, and their bodies began glowing a light blue. Multiple healing spells refilled their health to maximum instantly.

The next moment, numerous orange balls of fire shot up from behind the fortress of steel that was the line of shields, arching up toward the ceiling of the great cave chamber before plunging down on Kirito's location.

A great explosion turned the surface of the lake a deep red, swallowing the tiny black-clad figure.

"Kirito!" Leafa screamed. His HP bar plummeted all the way down to the yellow zone. In fact, given the extremely small variation in player HP values in ALO, it was a miracle it hadn't killed him outright. She'd never seen such a precise, concentrated magical attack. With a shiver, she suddenly understood the enemy's strategy.

They clearly knew that Kirito possessed an overwhelming physical attack, and they had concocted this tactic to counteract it.

The three heavies in the front made no move to attack. They simply held the line with their thick shields. No matter how powerful Kirito's sword was, it could not inflict a fatal blow if he never reached their bodies. The remaining nine behind them were probably all mages. Some of them focused on healing the guards, and the others rained down their projectile flames. It was the kind of formation players assumed to tackle a powerful boss monster.

But why? Why would such a large group assemble just to go after Kirito and Leafa?

Leafa put that question on the back burner as she queued up a healing spell. Kirito reappeared out of the dying flames, and she cast the best healing spell she knew. His HP bar started refilling immediately, but it was clear that this would not do much in the long run.

Kirito understood the enemy's strategy as well. Perhaps sensing that a protracted battle was unwinnable, he immediately swung back toward the shield-bearers, sword at the ready.

"Rahhh!!"

The gleaming black sword collided with the shields, sending out a blinding shower of sparks.

But the battle had already turned into a fatalistic numbers game.

The damage Kirito inflicted with each swing was recovered by the mages in the rear line and their healing spells. The next moment, the other mages cast their long-range attack spells, raining fire down upon him.

It was Leafa's least favorite kind of battle: locked in a pattern, with no room for personal ability to sway the outcome. The only factor that would determine this fight was whether the mages' mana or Kirito's health would run out first. The outcome was clear.

Yet another hail of fireballs enveloped Kirito. The deluge of orange light picked him up and threw him backward against the ground.

ALO did not re-create any kind of "pain" in its sensory feedback, but out of the sensations it did feature, a direct hit from explosive magic was one of the most unpleasant. A roar rocked the brain, the skin burned and prickled, and the sense of balance was hit with a shock wave. The effects could sometimes carry over to the real body, causing headaches and dizziness that lasted for several hours.

"*Rrh...aaagh!*"

But every time Kirito was hit, he got back to his feet and swung his sword again. Even as she helplessly chanted recovery spells, Leafa could feel his pain vicariously. It was just a game. Anyone would give up facing these odds. It hurt to lose, but given the mathematical systems underlying the game, there would just be times when it was numerically impossible to win. So why...?

Leafa couldn't stand to watch this keep happening to Kirito. She ran a few steps closer and shrieked, "It's all right, Kirito! It's only a few more hours of flight from Swilvane to start over! And we can buy again the items we lost. This is pointless!"

But Kirito barely turned his head, his voice low.

"No."

His eyes were red with the reflection of the fire surrounding them.

"As long as I'm alive, I won't stand to see a party member killed. It's the one thing I refuse to allow."

She was stunned into silence.

Different players had different reactions to an unwinnable situation. Some tried to awkwardly laugh it off, some shut their eyes and tensed up when the moment came, and some kept swinging wildly as long as they were able. But no matter the reaction, everyone who played the game gradually became accustomed to this virtual "death." It was an unavoidable part of playing a VRMMORPG, and each player had to find acceptance in his or her own way. Otherwise, the game wasn't a game.

But Leafa had never seen anything like the light that shone in Kirito's eyes. They were brimming with a fierce desire to overcome the impossible mathematical odds against the two warriors and find a path to survival. For an instant, she even forgot that they were inside a game, a virtual world.

"Raaahhh!!"

Kirito bellowed, setting the very air to rattling. In the instant that the enemy's fire relented, he made another reckless charge at the wall of shields. He dropped the sword to his right hand and made a fierce attempt with his left to grab the corner of a shield and pry it away. The salamander line broke at this unexpected move. He jammed his sword into the tiny space that opened in their defense.

Leafa had been playing the game since the start, and she'd never seen anything like this. He'd broken the line-of-shield defense at point-blank range without using any magic. It wasn't even a proper attack; it wouldn't do any real damage. But this act of apparent madness caused shouts of alarm from behind the wall.

"Damn! What does he think he's—?"

Suddenly, a quiet voice sounded in Leafa's ear. "Now's our only chance!"

She looked over to see Yui perched on her shoulder.

"Chance...?"

"The only uncertain variable is the enemy's mental state. Use all of your remaining mana to protect against the next attack, any way you can!"

"B-but that would be..."

Like spitting into the ocean, she couldn't finish. But Yui, supposedly just a rudimentary AI, was looking straight into her eyes with the same force of will she'd just seen from Kirito.

Leafa nodded in understanding and thrust her arms overhead.

The enemy mages were already chanting the next fireball spell. But it was slower than usual, perhaps because they were trying to time their release. She rattled off spellwords as fast as she could. One slip of the tongue and the entire spell would fizzle, but she didn't have a choice. Her lips and tongue moved as nimbly as they possibly could.

She was just an instant quicker to finish her cast. Countless tiny butterflies burst from her outstretched hands and enveloped Kirito's body.

The next moment, the enemy spell went off. Another wave of fireballs shot through the air, descending with a screech like a bombing raid. Flowers of fire landed on Kirito as he clung to the wall of shields.

"*Hrgh!*"

Leafa shielded her face from the pressure of the blast and gritted her teeth. Each time Kirito's protective magical field canceled out an exploding fireball, she lost a chunk off of her MP bar. Drinking a mana potion would never bring it back in time. Just as she was wondering what, if anything, this single act of protection was earning them, Yui yelled out in a piercing voice.

"Now, Papa!!"

Leafa trained her eyes forward with a start. Amid the crimson flames, Kirito stood up straight, sword at the ready. She could hear bits of spell chanting and consulted her memory to identify the words she caught.

But wasn't that…illusion magic?

She held her breath for a moment, then ground her teeth. Kirito was casting an illusion spell that turned a player's appearance into that of a monster. It was considered virtually useless in battle. A randomized process determined which monster, depending on the caster's attack power, but in most cases the result was a weak, unimpressive mob. Not only that, but since the player's statistics were not affected in any way, there was little to no fear from the transformation.

Leafa's mana had dropped precipitously until it was less than

10 percent. She'd followed Yui's lead on this roll of the dice, and the dice had failed her.

But she couldn't blame them. In a skill-heavy game like this, knowledge was the greatest part of strength. Kirito had only started in the past few days, and it would be cruel to expect him to understand the usefulness of each and every one of the countless spellwords in the game.

She put her last bit of strength into her hand. The final round of the enemy's fireballs would land at the same moment that her protective field died out. An even larger blast of fire erupted and slowly dissipated.

"Huh...?"

A wavering black shadow emerged from the wall of fire. For an instant, she thought her eyes were playing tricks on her. It was just too large to be right.

It was at least twice the height of the imposing salamanders. On a closer look, it appeared to be a giant, its back stooped.

"Is that...you, Kirito?" she mumbled. It was the only possibility. Clearly, this was Kirito's transformed figure after his illusion spell—but the *size*...

As Leafa stood transfixed, the black shadow slowly raised its head. It wasn't a giant. The head was elongated like a goat's, and two long, malevolent horns curved from the back. The round eyes glowed red, and flame breath licked between its fangs.

The pitch-black skin of its upper body was knotted with muscle, and its brawny arms were long enough to touch the floor. A sinewy, whiplike tail extended from its waist. The only word to describe its appearance was *demonic*.

The salamanders froze still, as though their souls had all been removed. The black demon slowly turned its head to the ceiling and roared.

"Groaaahh!!"

This time it wasn't hyperbole—the earth really did shake. Primal fear rose from the pit of their beings.

"Eeyaah!!"

One of the salamanders on the front line fell back a few steps, shrieking in terror. The monster darted forward with terrifying speed. A clawed hand slipped into the space between the shields, and a finger pierced the heavily armed warrior—and in the next instant, the salamander was gone, with only a red End Flame left in his place.

"Wha—?!"

The other two front salamanders uttered identical cries of alarm at seeing their partner felled in one blow. They lowered their shields and brandished their weapons left-handed, inching backward.

A furious shout arose from the mages in the rear, most likely from the group's leader.

"Don't break formation, you fools! It's only his appearance and reach! He can't damage us if you stay turtled up!"

But the warriors paid him no heed. The black demon roared deafeningly and pounced, gobbling the man on the right with its massive jaws and lifting the ones on the left in its claws. It dashed each of them fiercely, and two consecutive crunches signaled their end. The little red flames burst from their bodies like so much blood.

In the span of less than ten seconds, all three of the front warriors had been wiped out. Their leader regained his composure and barked out fresh commands, and the mages began casting anew. But these were pure mages, outfitted in no armor at all save red gloves—a far cry from the burly fighters who had manned the defense. The ebony demon hissing malevolent breath was having a far greater psychological effect than such spells ever managed, and the mages were terrified. Their casting speed was much slower than before.

Before they could finish the cast, the demon swiped viciously at the cluster of sorcerers. The two in front were helplessly tossed like rags, disintegrating into red fire mid-arc. The air was filled with the sound of screams and the breaking of glass. Without pause, the great trunk of its left arm snaked forward, and two more salamanders were cast aside.

The leader, recognizable by his more esoteric magical accessories, had once been safely in the middle of the pack, but now he was exposed, his gaunt face a rictus of panic. He fumbled his current spell, and the glow between his hands was snuffed into a cloud of black smoke.

Kirito's demon took a rumbling step forward and unleashed another bellow. The salamander leader made a little gasping cry and waved his hands helplessly. "R-retreat! Retrea—"

But he couldn't finish.

The demon crouched momentarily, then leaped forward. It landed in the midst of the huddled mages, the bridge shaking with the impact. What happened after that could not generously be called a "battle."

Each time the demon's claws swiped out, an End Flame resulted. One of them valiantly threw himself forward with his staff, but the beast's fangs devoured him from the top down before he could take a single swing.

The leader nimbly avoided the blast radius but promptly threw himself over the side of the bridge, evidently giving up the fight for lost. A fountain of water erupted where he landed, and he took off swimming with considerable speed for the far shore.

With total equipment underneath a certain weight level, there was no fear of sinking in ALO. This was good news for the mage, who sped off rapidly from the bridge—until an enormous shadow emerged under the water.

A moment later, there was a loud splash, and the leader disappeared beneath the surface. Only his breath bubbled up as the shadow descended into the depths. Before it vanished altogether, the faint glow of a red flame glimmered from below.

Kirito's demon showed no interest in the demise of the enemy leader. It raised the final, squealing victim in its hands, then pulled both ends as though wrenching him into two pieces.

Stunned into a trance at the scene of overwhelming violence, Leafa finally came back to her senses.

"No, Kirito! Leave him alive!" she shouted, racing over to

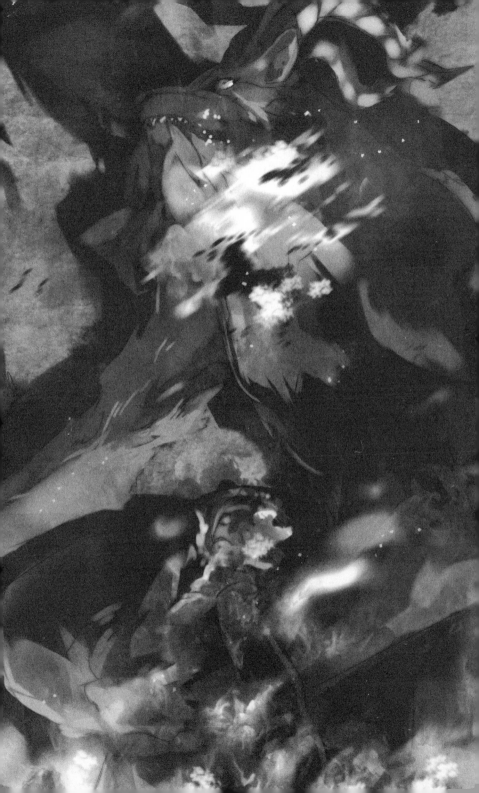

him while Yui nonchalantly remarked on the impressive spate of bloodshed that had just occurred. The demon stopped and turned, releasing the salamander's body in midair with a dissatisfied grunt.

The mage fell to the bridge with an unpleasant *splat* and writhed in silent shock, his mouth opening and closing. Leafa let her katana rest unpleasantly between his legs. The scrape of the tip against the cobblestone set him trembling.

"I want some answers! Who ordered you to do this?" she demanded in what she thought was her most menacing growl, but that only seemed to snap the man out of his shock. He shook his head, pale-faced.

"G-go ahead and kill me!"

"Why, you—"

Meanwhile, the demon that had been watching over this scene slowly began to disintegrate into a black mist. Leafa looked up to see a small figure emerge from the dissipating cloud and land on the bridge.

"Boy oh boy, that was a good rampage," Kirito said happily, cracking his neck and sheathing his sword over his back again. He crouched down next to the stunned salamander and patted the man's shoulder.

"Hey, that was a good fight."

"Huh…?"

He kept chatting with their helpless victim, his tone light. "It was a good strategy, it really was. If I were all alone, I wouldn't have stood a chance."

"Um, Kirito…"

"Hang on, I've got this." He winked at Leafa. "Now, we've got a deal to discuss."

Kirito pulled up a trade window and pointed out a list of items to the man. "Here's all the items and yrd I earned from this fight. If you answer the simple questions we have for you, I might just give you all of this loot. How about that?"

The man opened and closed his mouth several times, staring at

Kirito's bright smile. He glanced around the vicinity—probably checking to confirm that the period of resurrection for all the other salamanders had expired, and they'd been teleported back to their save point far from here—before looking back at Kirito.

"...Seriously?"

"Dead serious."

They traded devious smirks, and Leafa sighed to herself. "Men..."

"Very disappointing, isn't it?" Yui muttered from her shoulder. The two men exchanged nods of approval at the completion of their transaction, seemingly oblivious to the stares of disgust from the women.

Once the salamander started talking, he wouldn't stop.

"So earlier this evening, Gtacs— Oh, that's the leader of our mage squad. Anyway, he sent me a text saying to get into the game. I was eating dinner so I didn't want to go, but he said it was mandatory. So I come online, and we're putting together, like, more than a dozen people just to hunt down two? I was like, 'What kind of messed-up torture is this?' But then they said it was the people who took down Kagemune yesterday, so I was like, 'Oh...'"

"Who's Kagemune?"

"The captain of the lancers. He's an expert sylph hunter, so it was crazy when he got his butt whooped and had to turn tail and flee yesterday. That was you, right?"

Leafa shared a glance with Kirito, grimacing at the term *sylph hunter*. He was probably talking about the leader of the salamander squad they'd defeated the previous night.

"And what was this Gtacs doing, going after us?"

"It was an order from above him, apparently. Something about how you were an obstacle to the plan..."

"What plan?"

"I dunno, it's some big-time business for the big-time 'manders. They don't explain things to a guy like me way down on the totem pole, but it's something big, that's for sure. I saw a huge army of folks flying off to the north when I logged in."

"North..."

Leafa put a finger to her lips and thought. Gatan, the salamander capital, was on the very southern edge of Alfheim. A line drawn straight north from there would take them right to the very mountain range they were currently beneath. To the west was the entrance to the Lugru Corridor, and to the east was a gap in the mountains called the Dragon's Valley. Whichever direction they took, the next destination after that would be Alne, then the World Tree.

"Are you trying to conquer the World Tree?" Leafa asked.

He shook his head. "No way. We learned our lesson after the last disaster. We're saving up yrd to outfit everyone in the raid party with ancient weapons. They're forcing everyone to raise a huge quota...and we're not even halfway there yet."

"Hmm..."

"But that's all I know. You weren't lying about our deal, right?" he asked Kirito.

"A real man never lies when it comes to a deal," the spriggan boasted coolly. The salamander's face lit up in delight as he saw the stacks of items and cash slide into his trade window.

Leafa had choice words for the man. "Isn't that your friends' equipment? You don't feel guilty about taking it like this?"

He clucked his tongue. "You don't get it. They show off their rare stuff all the damn time—that's what makes this even sweeter. I'm not going to wear it, of course. I'll sell it all off and buy myself a house or something."

The salamander announced that he'd take a few days on the return trip, just to let the excitement cool down a bit, and took off in the direction they'd come.

Leafa stared at Kirito, who was back to his normal self, marveling at how the desperate battle they'd undergone not ten minutes before seemed to have never happened.

"Hmm? What's up?"

"Oh, er…That giant demon was you, right?" she asked. Kirito looked up and away, and then scratched his chin.

"Mmm, I guess so."

"You *guess* so…? Wasn't the entire plan to make the salamanders panic when they saw you as a monster?"

"Actually, I hadn't thought that far ahead…In fact, sometimes I just kind of snap in battle, and I lose all memory of what happens…"

"That's scary!"

"But I do kind of remember that just now. I used the spell like Yui suggested, and I felt myself getting really huge. And since I lost my sword, I just had to use my hands…"

"You were also chewing on them!" Yui added gleefully from Leafa's shoulder.

"Oh, right. You know, it was pretty fun getting to act like one of the monsters for once."

Leafa felt an insatiable curiosity rise inside of her, and she hesitantly spoke her question aloud.

"So, um…did the salamanders have…a flavor?"

"They definitely had the texture of barbecued meat when it gets just a little charred—"

"N-never mind, never mind!" She waved her hands in panic. He abruptly snatched one of them.

"*Grarh!*" he snarled, opening wide and popping her fingers into his mouth.

"Aaaaaargh!"

The surface of the underground lake rippled with Leafa's scream and the resulting smack.

"Ugh, oww…"

Kirito mumbled and trudged along, rubbing the cheek that Leafa had smacked with all her strength.

"That was your fault, Papa!"

"Tell me about it. How rude!"

Leafa and Yui were of one mind. Kirito pleaded his case, sulking like a scolded child.

"But I was just trying to make a witty, classy joke to break the ice after that terrifying battle..."

"Next time you'll taste my sword, not my fingers." Leafa shut her eyes and turned her face away, quickening her pace.

Before them loomed the massive stone gate, stretching all the way to the ceiling of the cavern. They had reached the entrance to Lugru, the mining city.

The plan was to spend a night here, to restock on supplies and gather intelligence about the latest developments. The unexpected battle on the bridge had eaten a lot of time, and it was nearly midnight in real life.

This was just the start of the busiest stretch of the day in ALO, but Leafa was a student, so she made sure to always log out by one o'clock. When she told Kirito, he thought for a moment, then nodded in understanding.

Through the gate, they were greeted by the clanging of hammers, as well as the lively accompaniment from the NPC musicians that served as game BGM.

The city itself was not very large, but it was an impressive sight; the rock walls lining the main thoroughfare were packed with clusters of stores and workshops hawking equipment, materials, food, and drinks. There was a surprising number of players crammed inside, and parties of relatively unfamiliar races like pookas and leprechauns passed by, laughing and chatting.

"So this is Lugru, huh...?"

Leafa couldn't help but marvel at the novelty of the bustling underground hub. She wandered over to the row of swords on display at the nearest storefront. Even the least friendly shopkeeper couldn't keep her from being excited about shopping.

She had just picked up a silver longsword from the stand to appraise it when Kirito spoke up from behind her. "By the way..."

"Hmm?"

"Didn't you get some kind of message when we were attacked by the salamanders? What was that about?"

"...Oh." Leafa spun around, her mouth agape. "I forgot."

She hurriedly opened a window and checked her message history. Even after rereading, Recon's warning made no sense. It could have just been an issue with his connection that cut off the end of it, but there were no signs of a follow-up.

In that case, she'd just have to ask him what he meant. But when Leafa tried to respond, Recon's name was grayed out on the friends list. He was already offline.

"Sheesh. Is he asleep?"

"Maybe you could check with him offline," Kirito suggested.

She didn't like bringing anything about Alfheim back to the real world with her. She didn't visit any of the ALO community sites, and she almost never discussed video games with Shinichi Nagata in real life.

But she couldn't deny that something about that mysterious message was eating away at her.

"Okay, can you wait here while I log off to check? Just watch over my body for a few minutes. And Yui?"

The little fairy was still sitting on her shoulder. "Yes?"

"Watch Papa closely so he doesn't try any funny business."

"Aye-aye!"

"Oh, come on!" Kirito wailed, affronted. Leafa gave him a mischievous chuckle and sat down on a nearby bench.

She opened her menu and hit the log-out button, her fourth trip of the day between worlds. Her mind began floating dizzily upward toward the real world far, far above.

"Whew..."

Suguha sighed deeply at the fatigue she felt rising from another long dive.

She rolled over on the bed, AmuSphere still on her head, to look at the alarm clock. Midori would be home very soon. Maybe she should stick around to say hello...

Suguha reached over blindly and fumbled for the cell phone she'd left on the headboard stand above her pillow. The phone's EL panel was integrated into its exterior finish. It spit out a list of messages that had arrived while she was in the game.

"What in the world?!"

Her eyes went wide. Twelve entries, all voice calls from Shin-ichi Nagata. The AmuSphere was configured so that calls of a certain priority—family, police, hospital—would automatically log out the player. Since Nagata didn't fall under that category, she'd missed all of these calls. But what was he calling about at this time of night?

She popped the phone open, preparing to call him back, when his thirteenth call of the evening flashed the shell of the phone bright blue. She hit a button and put the device to her ear.

"Hi, Nagata? What's going on?"

"Ah! Finally! What *took* you so long, Suguha?"

"Don't give me that attitude. Nothin' *happened*; I just got caught up in the game, 's all."

"L-listen, I've got bad news! Sigurd, he sold us out—not just us—he sold out Lady Sakuya, too!"

"Sold us out...? What do you mean? Start from the beginning."

"Ugh, there's no time...Okay, remember when the salamanders attacked us in the Ancient Forest yesterday? Didn't anything strike you as weird?"

Despite his apparent haste, Nagata had returned to his typical dragging speech. When he called her by her first name like that in person, she always convinced him to stop via a physical attack or two, but over the phone, she didn't have that option and had to put up with it.

The fact that the incident had only happened a day ago was somewhat of a shock to Suguha. It felt like she had met Kirito years and years ago.

"Huh? 'Weird'...? What happened?"

Kirito's entrance to the scene had left such an impression on her that the details of the air battle were fuzzy.

"When the group of eight salamanders set onto us, Sigurd said he would be a decoy, and he lured away three of them on his own, right?"

"Oh, now that you mention it...he didn't get away, did he?"

"He didn't. But thinking back on it, that wasn't the way Sigurd usually acts. Whenever he would split up the party, the decoy had to be someone else. He never let anyone else remain to lead the group. *Ever.*"

"Ahh...good point."

Sigurd's leadership skill in battle was unquestionable, but he was also tyrannical and controlling—he always had to be on top. It was utterly unlike him to sacrifice himself for the sake of his party members.

"But then...why would he do that?"

"That's the thing," Nagata said sourly. "He's working with the salamanders. Has been for a while, I suspect."

"*Huh?!*"

Now Suguha was well and truly shocked. She clenched the phone in her hand.

The power game conducted among the various races of ALO meant that spoof accounts for the purpose of spying were an everyday occurrence. There was no doubt that several of the sylphs who called Swilvane home were actually fake accounts run by players whose main avatar was a different race—particularly salamanders.

Because of this, natural barriers arose—low-skill, low-contribution, low-activity players were never admitted to the center of power, due to the high likelihood of espionage. It wasn't that long ago that even Leafa wasn't allowed into the lord's mansion behind the Tower of Wind.

But since the dawning of ALO, Sigurd had been heavily active in sylph politics. He had been a nominee in all four of the lord elections to this point. He was always a runner-up due to the overwhelming popularity of the current leader, but even after losing, he played the role of a valuable adviser. In short, he was an irreplaceable piece of sylph power.

It was almost impossible to believe that he could be spying for the salamanders.

"Oh, come on...do you have any proof of that?" she asked, her voice low.

"I had a hunch, so I went hollow this morning and shadowed Sigurd all day long."

"...You really have nothing better to do, do you?"

He was referring to Hollow Body, an invisibility trick of Recon's. Only those who had mastered both high-level concealment magic and the Sneaking skill could use it.

Recon took his player handle from the American military shorthand for "reconnaissance"—although he pronounced it "reckon" rather than "ree-con." He'd designed his character for the purpose of scouting during hunts, which made him suited to tracking as well. He once made use of those skills to follow Leafa back into the inn room where she was staying, claiming that he was only going to leave her a surprise birthday present and leave without drawing any attention. He was beaten half to death for that crime.

Nagata continued, ignoring the exasperation in her voice.

"After the horrible stuff he said to you in the Tower of Wind, I was looking for a chance to poison him dead. And what did I see—"

"Oh my God, you're crazy."

"—but Sigurd and his pals putting on invisibility cloaks and vanishing. I knew they were up to something. They can try to sneak off, but mere items can't fool me."

"Enough of the bragging. What happened next?"

"They went into the sewers. After about five minutes of walking, there were these two fishy-looking folks waiting for them. They had invisibility cloaks, too, and when they took them off, would you believe it? They were salamanders!"

"What? But those cloaks don't fool the NPC guardians, right? They would have been cut down the moment they walked into town. Unless..."

"Exactly. Unless they had Pass Medallions."

Pass Medallions were special items given to individual visitors of another race when entering a home territory, and only after a stringent security check. They were only issued by the highest officers of each race and, once given, were non-transferrable. Who had the ability to give them out? Sigurd, of course.

"I knew I'd caught them red-handed. I listened in and heard the salamanders saying they'd put a tracer on you, Leafa. And not only that...the reason Lady Sakuya was away from home today was because she was meeting with the cait siths in a secret neutral location to discuss an alliance."

"Ahh...so that's why the flag at the mansion was down."

Nagata shouted over her murmur of understanding. "Sigurd's going to have a battalion of salamanders...attack the signing ceremony!"

"Wha—"

Suguha's breath caught in her throat. She was prepared to leave it behind forever, but the sylph territory was still her home, and Sakuya was a benevolent leader. She unleashed her rising panic into the speaker.

"Y-you should have said so earlier! This is bad news!"

"That's exactly what I said when you finally picked up the phone," Nagata sulked. She cut him off before he kept whining.

"Well, did you tell Sakuya? There's still time, right?"

"I knew it was big trouble, so I turned around to leave the sewer, and I accidentally kicked a rock..."

"You klutz! You idiot!"

"...You know, these days it kind of feels good when you yell at me, Suguha..."

"*Sicko!!* What then? Did you get in touch with her?"

"The salamanders' searcher stripped away my hiding spell. I wasn't that worried, because I figured if they killed me, I'd just revive at the tower and run right into the lord's mansion. But then they hit me with poison darts! Isn't that messed up?"

This didn't fly with what he'd said earlier, but she didn't have time to bother with that.

"So...where are you now...?"

"The salamanders have me held prisoner in the sewer, paralyzed...There was nothing else I could do, so I logged out and tried to call you, but you wouldn't pick up, and I don't know how to contact anyone else in real life...Oh yeah, and they said the meeting with the cait sith leader is at one o'clock...Aww man, we only have forty minutes left! Wh-what should we do, Suguha?!"

She sighed deeply and spoke quickly.

"Do you know where the meeting is?"

"Not the precise coordinates...but it's apparently past the Butterfly Valley on the other side of the mountains."

"Got it. I'll find a way to get there and warn them. I've got to hang up now to do that."

"Wait, Suguha!" Nagata's panicked voice stopped her finger at the button.

"What?"

"Umm, so, what's going on with you and that Kirito guy?"

Click.

She hung up without answering and tossed the phone back onto her headboard, then closed her eyes and stuffed her face into her pillow. She said the one magic spellword at her disposal in real life, and then headed back into the world of plots and conspiracies.

Leafa jumped back to her feet the instant her eyes opened.

"Whoa, you scared me!!"

The black-clad spriggan nearly dropped the mysterious food he must have bought at a nearby stand—it looked like a skewer of small grilled reptiles—but he caught it in time.

"Hi again, Leafa."

"Welcome back."

Leafa didn't have time to return Kirito and Yui's greetings.

"Kirito—I'm sorry."

"Uh, about what?"

"I have urgent business I need to see to right now, and I don't have time to explain. I don't think I'll be able to make it back."

"..."

He looked straight into her eyes for a moment and promptly nodded in understanding. "Okay. You can explain while we move."

"Huh...?"

"Either way, you'll need to use your feet to get out of this place, right?"

"...Fine. I'll talk as we run."

Leafa took off down the main street of Lugru, looking for a corner that would put her in the direction of Alne. They wound their way through the crowds and under a large gate carved out of a giant boulder. It spit them out on another stone bridge crossing another underground lake. Leafa filled in Kirito on the details as they ran, boots clacking on the stones. It was very fortunate that there was no fear of running out of breath in ALO.

"...I see." When Leafa was done talking, Kirito looked ahead, deep in thought. "Mind if I ask a few things?"

"Go ahead."

"What do the salamanders get by attacking the leaders of the sylphs and cait siths?"

"Well, first, they can prevent the alliance. The cait siths won't be happy at all if their lord gets whacked because the sylphs leaked the information. In a worst-case scenario, it might even lead to war between the two... The salamanders are currently the most powerful faction in the game, but if the sylphs and cait siths join forces, they'll probably flip the power balance. The salamanders want to prevent that from happening."

They reached the other side of the bridge and entered another cave tunnel. Leafa set her map to display in front of her so she could check their path as they ran.

"Also, you get a massive bonus for defeating an enemy lord. You earn thirty percent of all the gold stockpiled in that lord's mansion. Not only that, but the mansion's city is considered occupied for ten days, and all players can be taxed freely. It's an incredible amount of gold we're talking about. And the reason the salamanders are the most powerful now is because they managed to kill the original sylph lord with a trap. Lords almost never, ever leave the safety of home territory because of it. That was the only time any lord has ever been killed in ALO."

"I see..."

"That's why, Kirito." She glanced over at the profile of the boy running beside her. "This is a sylph problem... You don't have any reason to get further involved. Alne is just on the other side once we exit this cave. I'm guessing we wouldn't leave the meeting place alive, so we'd have to start over from Swilvane all over again, which is a waste of several more hours of gameplay. And in fact..."

Leafa had to shut something tight in her heart in order to say what came next.

"If you really need to get to the top of the World Tree, your best bet might be working with the salamanders. If their plot succeeds, they'll have more than enough money to make a solid attempt on the World Tree. Maybe they'll hire a spriggan as a mercenary—I'm not going to complain if you just kill me right here."

I won't resist it if that happens, she thought. It was unfathomable under normal circumstances, but she knew she couldn't beat him, and she didn't want to fight him, even if they'd only known each other for a single day.

If it comes to that... I might even quit ALO altogether...

She looked over at Kirito again, who was still running, his expression unchanged.

"Anything goes; it's just a game. Kill what you want, take what you want," he muttered, then paused. "I've seen enough people who think that way to last a lifetime. In a way, it's true—I used to think that way myself. But it's not. There are things you have to protect and uphold *because* it's a virtual world, even if it makes you look stupid. I learned that from someone…very important to me…"

His voice suddenly turned warm and gentle.

"It might seem like a paradox, but I don't think you can fully isolate the player from the role-playing in this VRMMO thing. If you let your inner greed run wild in this world, that will come back to haunt your real-life personality. The player and character are one and the same. I like you, Leafa. I want to be your friend. I would never cut down someone I liked for personal gain, no matter the reason."

"Kirito…"

Leafa stopped running, her breath suddenly trapped in her chest. A moment later, Kirito stopped as well.

She clenched her hands together, trying to stay upright in the indescribable deluge of emotion engulfing her, and looked into his black eyes.

Oh…I see, she thought.

It was the reason she always kept a certain distance from every other player in this game. She couldn't tell if she was dealing with a flesh-and-blood human being or a character in a game. Behind every word, she couldn't help but wonder what people were really thinking. She didn't know how to respond to others, and every outstretched hand became a weight on her shoulders, something she could only escape with the beat of her wings.

But there was no need for her to bother with that. Let her heart feel as it felt. That was all she needed, and that was the only truth.

"…Thank you."

The words floated up from the deepest part of her heart. If she tried to say anything else, she knew she would burst into tears.

Kirito smiled shyly. "Sorry, I didn't mean to preach at you there. It's a bad habit."

"No, I truly appreciate it. So…I guess this is good-bye, once we leave the cave."

Kirito's eyebrows popped up in surprise. "No, I'm going with you, of course."

"H-huh?"

"Oh crap, I'm using up your time, aren't I? Can you navigate while we run, Yui?"

"Roger that!" the diminutive fairy squeaked. He turned back to Leafa.

"Can I see your hand?"

"Umm..."

Kirito reached out with his left hand and squeezed Leafa's right. Even in her confusion, Leafa's heart leaped when she realized it was the first time they'd held hands. In the next instant, Kirito took off at ferocious speed. A shock wave rattled her eardrums, as though they were breaking through a wall of air.

She thought they'd been running fast before, but it was nothing like this. They were moving so fast, the texture of the rock walls melted into radial blurs. With Kirito dragging her by the hand, Leafa felt her body float nearly horizontal in the air, flopping left and right whenever he took a sharp turn through the tunnels. It was the least romantic experience in the world.

"Whaaa—?!"

She couldn't help but wail and squint her eyes as they passed through a wider space in the cave. A large number of yellow cursors blinked into life around them—they'd disturbed a pack of orcs.

"Um, um, monsters—" she tried to yell, but Kirito plunged straight through the group without any sign of slowing down.

"Aaaaah!"

Leafa's scream met the roar of the monsters'. But the crude knives they swung at her did not land a single blow. Kirito instantly identified the spaces among them and weaved his way through with frightening speed. The orcs screeched and hissed with anger, but by the time they turned to pursue, Kirito and Leafa were already down the next tunnel.

They disturbed a few more packs of orcs, but Kirito never stopped running. Naturally, this caused a large horde of monsters to gather in hot pursuit, the ground behind them rumbling like the sound of river rapids. This phenomenon was called "running a train" and was considered quite poor manners. Any fellow players they ran across would no doubt be swallowed by the mass of orcdom trailing behind the pair, but fortunately they had no such encounters before the light of day grew visible at the end of the cave.

"Hey, that might be the exit," Kirito said, moments before Leafa's vision went pure white. Suddenly, her feet were no longer touching earth.

"*Hyieeeeh?!*"

She squeezed her eyes shut and screeched, her legs flapping in open air, until she realized that the roaring that had enveloped her body for the last few minutes had dissipated.

When she found the courage to open her eyes again, they were in the midst of endless sky. Kirito must have taken them straight out of the cave exit and halfway up the mountain at full speed, launching them into the air like a catapult. Below her feet was nothing but sheer gray cliffs. Their momentum was taking them up into a majestic parabola through the air.

She hastily spread her wings to enter a controlled glide, and she finally let out the breath she'd been holding.

"*Bwah!*"

Wheezing and panting, she turned back to look at the shrinking cave mouth and saw with a shiver that it was packed with monsters. She gave Kirito her nastiest glare.

"You shortened my lifespan!"

"Ha-ha, I think you mean I shortened our trip time!"

"Dungeon-crawling is supposed to be a careful process where you isolate monsters and keep them from ganging up on you... I don't know what game you're playing, but it's not this one," she muttered. Eventually, her pulse returned to normal, and she took a fresh look at their surroundings.

Directly below was a vast meadow with the occasional lake sparkling in the sun. A winding river connected those pools of blue, and beyond that was...

"Oh…"

Leafa held her breath.

A vast, vague shadow loomed beyond the sea of clouds above. The trunk reached into the heights like a pillar bearing the very sky itself, and the branches and leaves that sprouted at the top were large as constellations.

"So that's…the World Tree," Kirito murmured in amazement at her side.

Just out of the mountains, they were a good twelve miles of real distance from the tree, but it dominated that stretch of the sky already. It was impossible to imagine what it would be like to stand at its base.

They floated onward for several moments, staring at the World Tree in silence, before Kirito came to his senses.

"Hey, we can't just be sitting here. Where's this big meeting taking place, Leafa?"

"Oh, good point. Well, the mountain range we just crossed forms a giant circle around the center of the world map. There are three major passes through the mountains: Dragon's Valley, facing salamander land; Rainbow Valley, facing the undines'; and Butterfly Valley, next to the cait siths'. They're holding the meeting on the interior side of Butterfly Valley, so…"

She wheeled around until she pointed northwest. "We'll need to fly in that direction for a bit."

"Gotcha. How much time do we have?"

"…Twenty minutes."

"So if the salamanders are attacking the meeting, they'll go from here to there," he surmised, waving his hand from southeast to northwest. "We don't know if they're ahead of us or behind, so I guess we just have to hurry and hope for the best. Let us know of any big groups you detect within search radius, Yui."

"Okay!"

All on the same page, they beat their wings and picked up speed.

*   *   *

"Funny, why aren't there any monsters?" Kirito wondered aloud as they cut through the clouds.

"Oh, there are no monsters on the Alne Plateau. I suppose that's why they chose it for the meeting."

"I see. Kind of ruins the scene, if your big diplomatic gathering is interrupted by a monster attack...Doesn't help us much now, though."

"What do you mean?"

Kirito flashed her a wicked grin. "I could have piled up another train of monsters and led them right into the salamander raid party."

"Where do you get ideas like this? The salamanders are going to be in an even larger party than the one that attacked us in the cave, so either our warning will be in time and everyone will flee to safety in cait sith land, or they'll kill us all together."

"..."

Kirito rubbed his chin, thinking hard.

"Oh! Player signal!" Yui suddenly cried. "A large gathering ahead—sixty-eight in total. I believe this is the salamander raid. There are another fourteen farther ahead, most likely the participants in the sylph–cait sith meeting. The two groups will meet in roughly fifty seconds."

Just as she finished her announcement, the cloud cover blocking their view ended. Leafa was at the maximum possible flying altitude, and there was green grassland below.

Far below them was a group of countless figures. They flew in distinct, five-man wedges, and their silent, careful progress made them look like menacing stealth bombers closing in on a hapless, oblivious target.

She looked farther beyond in the direction they flew and spied a small, circular terrace. That white strip in the middle must have been the long table. There were seven chairs on either side, making it an impromptu meeting room.

The people seated at the table must have been deep in conversation, as they showed no sign of noticing the coming threat.

"We didn't make it," Leafa mumbled to Kirito.

Even if they somehow sped past the salamanders to warn the two leaders, not all of them would make it to safety in time. She had to be prepared to sacrifice herself and act as a shield to allow the leaders to escape.

She reached out her hand and softly held Kirito's.

"Thank you, Kirito. This is far enough. You go to the World Tree...It wasn't that long, but it was certainly fun," she said with a smile. But just as she tucked her wings and prepared for a steep dive, Kirito squeezed back. She looked up with a start and saw his usual confident smile.

"Running out isn't my style."

He let go and plopped Yui back into his shirt pocket, then beat his wings hard and sped ahead. Leafa had to close her eyes for an instant, as a brief shock wave hit her full in the face. When she opened them again, Kirito was already in a dive, headed straight for the little terrace.

"W-wait?! What are you doing?!" Leafa shouted, slightly hurt that her meaningful farewell had been ruined in an instant. But Kirito did not turn back. She hurried after him, exasperated.

Ahead, the sylphs and cait siths had finally noticed the brigade descending upon them. They kicked chairs aside and drew blades, the silver flashing in the sun, but compared to the heavily armed assault squad, they were woefully underpowered.

The lead team of low-flying salamanders surged suddenly upward and halted, readying their long lances like birds of prey about to descend on a rabbit. Further teams flanked right and left, until they half surrounded the terrace. The world was blanketed in the moment of silence before slaughter.

One of the salamanders raised a hand. Just as he was about to give the signal to attack—

An enormous cloud of dust erupted at the edge of the terrace directly between the opposing sides. A split second later, the air rocked with the sound of an explosion. Kirito, the black meteorite, had crashed to Earth without slowing a bit.

Every person in the clearing froze. The dust slowly settled and Kirito got to his feet, turning to stare imperiously at the salamanders, hands on his hips. He puffed out his chest, took a deep breath—

"Stay your blades, all of you!!"

"Whoa!"

Even in her dive, Leafa cringed. The shout was so deafening, the previous explosion might as well have been whisper-quiet. She was a few dozen yards up in the air still, and her body was tingling with the force of it. The salamander formation shook as though suffering some kind of physical pressure, the members falling back on their heels.

The volume of his voice was one thing, but his astonishing nerve was another. What in the world did he think he was going to accomplish here?

Despite the trickle of sweat down her back, Leafa landed behind Kirito, next to the green-clad sylphs. She soon found one in a very recognizable outfit.

"Sakuya," she called out. The sylph turned at the sound, and her dazed eyes went wide.

"Leafa? What are you doing h—? I mean, what's happening?"

She'd never seen the leader of the sylphs so unraveled. "It's a long story. The short version is that our fate is currently in his hands."

"...I'm so confused..."

The sylph turned her back on Leafa and watched the proud, dark figure. Leafa took the opportunity to sneak a good look at Sakuya—Lady Sakuya, the leader of the sylphs.

She was extremely tall for a sylph woman, her straight hair—such a dark shade of green it was nearly black—falling long down her back and cut cleanly straight across. Her skin was so white you could almost see through it, her eyes were long and slender, her nose was graceful, and her lips were small and thin. Hers was the kind of beauty that cut like a knife.

She wore a traditional front-opening kimono. Tucked inside the sash was a lengthy katana, even longer than Leafa's. Her pure white legs ended in tall wooden sandals that were red. The overall effect was stunning, and this memorable appearance had helped her win nearly 80 percent of the vote in the elections.

But those votes were not all cast for her beauty, of course. The business of leading an entire race of players kept her from hunting, so her statistics were not as high as others. But she was skilled enough with the blade to reach the final in nearly any dueling tournament. She was also honest and forthright, and she commanded respect.

It was then that Leafa noticed a petite woman standing next to Sakuya.

The large, triangular ears poking out from her wavy, corn-gold hair were the signature mark of a cait sith. She exposed plenty of wheat-brown skin through her swimsuit-like battle outfit. On either side of her waist were clawlike melee weapons with three massive talons each. A long striped tail extended from the rear of her suit, and it twitched and trembled as though expressing its owner's anxiety.

She had large eyes with long lashes and a small, rounded nose—features that almost seemed a bit too adorable, but which certainly made her stand out from the standard look of ALO. Leafa had never met her before, but she could guess that this was Alicia Rue, lady of the cait siths. Like Sakuya, her extraordinary popularity had made her a longtime leader of her people.

Behind the two fairy leaders were sylphs and siths, six each on either side of the long white table, all looking stunned by this turn of events. She'd never seen any of the cait siths, of course, but all the sylphs were high-ranking players. She checked just in case, and, sure enough, there was no sign of Sigurd.

By the time she turned back to the southern end of the terrace and its salamanders, Kirito was shouting again.

"I wish to speak with your commander!"

The salamander lancers, bowled over by his bold manner and voice, parted ways. A single large warrior proceeded through the empty space.

He had short red hair, spiked straight upward; burnt brown skin; and a sharp, hawkish face. His brawny body was clad in reddish-bronze armor that was clearly of extremely rare quality, and on his back was a sword every bit as large as Kirito's.

When she looked into the red fire burning in his eyes, a shiver ran down Leafa's back, even though she wasn't face-to-face with him. She'd never seen a player with such overwhelming presence.

He landed heavily in front of Kirito and glared down at the little black swordsman, his face expressionless. After a long moment like that, he opened his mouth, and a deep voice rumbled out.

"What are you doing here, spriggan? We will kill you, no matter the answer, but in light of your audacity, I will hear you out."

Kirito answered loudly, unfazed.

"I am Kirito, an envoy of the spriggan-undine alliance. May I presume your attack upon this scene is meant as open war against all four of our races?"

Oh, no.

Leafa couldn't speak. It was preposterous; the worst bluff she'd ever heard. It was no longer a trick of her mind—actual sweat was running down her back. Despite the obvious shock on her face, she tried to give Sakuya and Alicia Rue a reassuring wink.

Even the commander of the salamanders was taken aback.

"An alliance between undines and spriggans...?" But he soon regained his composure. "And you are their envoy, without a single guard at your back?"

"That's right. I was only here for trade negotiations with the sylphs and cait siths. But if you attack this meeting, there will be much more than that. All four races will be forced to join together to oppose you."

The world was silent for several moments. Eventually...

"I cannot take the word of a single man at face value, especially one with no real equipment."

The salamander reached behind his back and loudly drew his double-sided blade. The metal gleamed dark and red, two entwined dragons inlaid on the flat of the sword.

"If you can withstand thirty seconds of my attacks, I will believe that you are an envoy."

"Very generous of you," Kirito responded lightly, drawing his own giant sword. This one was a dull gray with no ornamentation.

He vibrated his wings and rose to hover at the same height as the salamander. In an instant, it seemed as though the space between them sparked hot and white with pure, murderous focus.

... Thirty seconds passed...

Leafa gulped audibly.

From what she'd seen of Kirito's skill, those conditions were certainly winnable. But the sheer lethality radiating from the salamander commander was considerable.

Amid the tense silence, Sakuya quietly muttered at Leafa's side.

"This is bad..."

"Huh...?"

"I've seen that salamander's two-handed sword on a site detailing the legendary weapons of the game. It's the Demon Blade Gram... which would mean he must be General Eugene. Know him?"

"I've... heard the name..." Leafa returned, holding her breath. At that, Sakuya continued.

"He's the younger brother of Lord Mortimer of the salamanders... They're apparently actual brothers in real life. His brother's got the brains, and he's got the brawn. People say Eugene's better when it comes to pure fighting power. He's the strongest of all the salamanders... which would make him..."

"The strongest player in the game?"

"Quite possibly... We've really got a situation on our hands."

"...Oh, Kirito..."

Leafa clenched her hands to her chest.

In midair, as though measuring each other's true strength, the two fighters glared at each other for a long time. The clouds hanging low over the plateau broke here and there, sending angled pillars of sunlight across the scene. One caught the salamander's blade, flashing vividly.

Without warning, Eugene sprang into motion.

He launched into an ultra-speed charge, the air rebounding around him. The greatsword to his right traced a wide red arc down onto the small spriggan.

But Kirito's reaction was just as fast. He held his sword over his head without any wasted motion and spread his wings, ready for the attack. Leafa could see his intent: He would deflect the enemy's sword and strike back in quick succession. But—

"—?!"

The instant the red sword descending on Kirito met the black sword, it grew hazy and indistinct. It passed directly through Kirito's sword and went solid again.

Dagaaang!! The world shook with the explosion. The slash caught Kirito square in the chest with a massive flash, and his slender form struck the ground like a leaf caught in the midst of a storm gale. There was another blast and a cloud of dirt.

"Wh-what was that?" Leafa said, stunned. Alicia Rue had the answer.

"Demon Blade Gram has a unique extra effect called Ethereal Shift, which allows it to pass through any sword or shield that tries to block it!"

"No way..."

She looked closer, hoping to call up Kirito's HP bar. But before the game could detect her line of sight and show a cursor, a shadow shot out of the dirt cloud like an arrow. It careered straight for the hovering Eugene.

"Well, well...you survived the hit!" the salamander crowed, delighted.

"What the hell was that?" Kirito shouted back, striking with his sword in response.

Kaang, clang! The clashes rang out in succession. Eugene was not just blessed with an excellent weapon; he used his bulky sword to deflect each and every one of those attacks of Kirito's that Leafa herself had never been able to follow.

Once that combination finally abated for an instant, it happened again.

The Demon Blade Gram exposed its fangs. Kirito instinctually tried to block the sideways swipe with his own sword, and once again it blurred and struck him deep in the gut.

"Gaaah!!"

It sounded like all of the air in his lungs had been expelled outward. Spinning, he flew up into the air and only stopped his momentum with his wings at full brake.

"That stings...Hasn't it been thirty seconds already?" Kirito wailed. Eugene smiled confidently.

"Sorry, now I want to kill you. This lasts until I've made you my trophy."

"Son of a bitch...Can't wait to see the tears in your eyes."

Kirito hoisted his massive sword again, but the fight seemed as good as over.

Parrying was not an option to defend against Gram's extra effect—the only way was to avoid it entirely. But that was nearly impossible with the lightning-fast blows in the battle.

Sakuya must have come to the same conclusion. "It'll be tough...Their skill as players seems about equal, but the weapons are hardly so. The only weapon that can counteract a unique-level demon blade would be another legendary weapon, the Holy Blade Excalibur, but no one even knows where to get it," she said.

"..."

If anyone could do it, Kirito could. He's barely played this game for a day, and yet he's used his unfathomable skill to overturn impossible odds over and over, Leafa told herself, clutching her hands to her chest.

Eugene thrust sharply, red light streaming from his wings. Kirito swung wide at a random angle and just barely dodged.

The two fairies wound through the air in complicated patterns, occasionally colliding in vivid bursts of visual effects, then separating again. Kirito's HP bar was under the halfway point after the two direct hits he'd taken. Not too long ago, she'd seen Kirito defend himself against a withering magic assault, and yet Eugene had pierced that stout defense easily. He was the real deal.

Kirito suddenly spun and stuck out his right hand. He must have been chanting spellwords, because his hand flashed black—

Boom, boomboomboom! Clouds of smoke erupted around them. The area-of-effect illusion spell expanded until it covered a wide radius.

The black clouds hovered over the heads of everyone on the ground, plunging the area into a sudden darkness. Leafa squinted to try to make out Kirito's figure, even as her field of vision grew dim.

"Leafa, I need this for a moment."

"Wha—?!"

She yelped as a voice whispered in her ear. She could sense her beloved katana being removed from its sheath. "K-Kirito?"

Leafa spun around, but no one was there. Her sheath, however, was empty.

"Is this your idea of buying time?" Eugene's shout emerged from the midst of the thick smoke. It was followed by the sound of spell chanting.

A wave of red light flicked outward through the black. The dispel effect worked quickly, removing the smoke and returning light to the vicinity.

Leafa looked up hastily to the sky above. But—

He was gone.

Only the lone salamander general floated in the air. No matter where she looked, she saw no short, nimble spriggan.

"You don't think…he took off to save his own skin?" a cait sith mumbled behind her. Leafa spun and shouted before the sentence had finished.

"He wouldn't!!"

He would never. Even in this situation, when almost any player would turn and run for his life, *he* wouldn't.

The boy named Kirito wasn't just "playing" this VRMMO. He was living it. He saw this virtual world as another reality of its own, and he believed in the truth of the trust, bonds, and love that grew out of it.

Can you hear it? There.

A beautiful, high-pitched flight tone, almost like a flute. It grew closer. Louder, louder.

"…!!"

When Leafa finally caught sight of him, tears blurred the sight.

He was in the sun—the brightest source of game light in Alfheim. In a rapid line, one small shadow descended, through the brilliant rays pouring down from above.

A few moments later than Leafa, Eugene looked straight up. But the effect of the sunlight caused him to grimace and raise his hand to block it. A normal player might have tried to move laterally to avoid the sun and been battered from directly above.

But Eugene was no normal player. His broad mouth grimaced, then gaped wide.

"Daaaahh!"

With a shout that rocked the earth, he launched the salamander's signature charge attack directly into the sun. His body shot upward like a rocket, a vertical beam of red light trailing in his wake.

As Kirito plunged down from above, he'd switched the two-handed grip on his giant sword to his right hand, for some reason. His left hand was held behind him, out of sight.

Suddenly he held it aloft, shining brilliantly in the midst of the sun's sizzling beams.

Leafa couldn't have mistaken the silver gleam in his hand if she'd tried. It was the katana Kirito had taken from her scabbard just moments ago. He was wielding a sword in each hand.

The concept of dual blades wasn't new. But despite the number of players who'd attempted such a style, Leafa knew of none who had succeeded in making it work. It was simply far too difficult to wield two with the kind of precision needed to win in battle.

In real-world kendo matches, it wasn't against the rules to wield two *shinai*, one large and one small. But it was forbidden in official competition in middle and high school, and very few practitioners used them in college and above. It was simply too hard to use two swords to effectively strike a legal target and receive a point. The same could be said of using two blades in this virtual world.

Eugene smirked confidently, seeing Kirito's choice of equipment as a last-ditch desperation choice.

But Leafa, her wide eyes filled with tears, believed with all her heart.

The salamanders' demonic blade roared heavily upward. The spriggan brought down his silver katana to meet it.

The red-and-black blade vibrated. The Ethereal Shift effect took it straight through toward Kirito's neck—

Gying! The tip of the sword was knocked back with a sharp crash. Kirito had stopped it with the massive sword in his right hand, just in the nick of time. The timing was perfect, as precise as threading a needle.

As Eugene's eyes went wide with shock, Kirito unleashed a thunderous bellow.

"Uuua...*aaaahhhh!!*"

The swords in his hands shot forward so fast, they were nothing but a blur.

The katana sliced smoothly. The greatsword thrust forward, the two exchanging like pistons. He pulled back and went in again, the katana flying forward from the lower left. As though drawn to the same trajectory, the greatsword pounded heavily after it.

Silver and black melted together. The consecutive blows were like shooting stars in the night sky. Leafa couldn't imagine the length of training required to wield two swords with such speed and precision. Even as he was pushed back, Eugene tried valiantly to use his sword's shifting attacks to counter, but it did not seem to work in succession against multiple blades, and he was rebuffed by the double-parry every time.

"Nraahhh!!"

General Eugene roared as he was pushed farther back to earth. One of the pieces of armor he wore exhibited a special effect, forcing out a half-spherical field of fire that pushed Kirito back a bit. He instantly readied his demon sword for a pure, massive swing.

Gong! He struck straight forward with a deafening crash.

Kirito showed no sign of fear, dashing to close the distance, swinging the katana as fast as lightning.

Shang! rang out a high-pitched metallic clash. Vivid sparks arched through the air.

The katana struck the side of the sword before it could activate the Ethereal Shift, and Eugene's blow grazed Kirito's left shoulder on its way past him.

"Raaahhhh!!"

Kirito's enormous sword leaped forward with tremendous force.

Thud! The dark blade pierced the salamander's body.

"Gwaah!"

The impossible speed of Kirito's thrust and the momentum of both men moving in opposite directions gave the strike incredible damage. Eugene's HP bar instantly plunged into the yellow zone.

But Kirito did not stop there. He quickly pulled back the larger sword and transitioned into another katana slash faster than the eye could follow, even as Eugene attempted to regain attack footing. The visual paths of the four blows, all struck in the space of a single breath, left a beautiful square in midair, enveloping the salamander's heavy body.

"...!!"

A look of shock painted across his face, Eugene found his upper half sliding silently from right shoulder to left waist. The light of Kirito's square filtered away.

The man's massive frame was suddenly awash in End Flames, his avatar burning away.

Not a single person moved.

The sylphs, the cait siths, and the fifty-plus salamanders were frozen in place, as though their souls had left their bodies.

That was just how high-level a battle they'd witnessed.

The typical fight in ALO was an ugly thing; close-range fighters swung their weapons awkwardly and long-range mages tossed off spells with little fanfare or strategy. Only a small handful of experienced players had any skill at defense or evasion. The only times anyone was likely to see a truly graceful battle was in the closing matches of a dueling tournament.

But what they'd just seen between Kirito and Eugene was far and above even that.

A flowing sword dance, a high-speed air duel, and, most vividly of all, Eugene's earth-splitting blows against Kirito's light-speed dual blades...

Sakuya broke the silence first.

"Well done, well done!" she applauded firmly, clapping her hands vigorously.

"That was amazing! What a great fight!" Alicia Rue joined in, and the other twelve soon followed. They clapped, cheered, whistled, and cried, "Bravo!"

Exhilarated but nervous, Leafa watched the army of salamanders. After the way their leader was beaten, she figured they would be rattled.

But to her surprise, the wave of cheers infected the salamander ranks as well. A great cheer broke out, and they hoisted their lances and waved them like flagpoles.

"Wow...!"

She finally let a smile cross her face.

Her enemy—salamanders she'd thought no better than lawless plunderers—were still fellow players of ALO. The excitement of Kirito and Eugene's duel had touched their hearts just as it had hers.

Overcome by a very strange sensation, Leafa joined in the rapturous applause.

Standing in the center of the adulation, Kirito wore his usual aloof smile. He returned the sword to his back and raised a hand in greeting.

"Hi, folks! Thanks!"

He repeated the gesture in all directions, then shouted toward Leafa's group. "Someone cast a resurrection spell!"

"Very well," Sakuya said, approaching. The dangling folds of her outfit rippled as she rose to the level of Eugene's Remain Light and began chanting the words.

Eventually, blue light spilled from her hands and surrounded the red flame. It formed into a complex magical sigil, and in the center, the flame gradually turned back into the form of a person.

The sigil gave one final flash before disappearing. Kirito, Sakuya, and the revived Eugene silently descended to the edge of the terrace. The scene was quiet once again.

"Your skill is unparalleled. I've never seen a better player," Eugene said quietly.

"Thanks," Kirito quipped.

"I'd no idea the spriggans had a man like you on their side... The world's a bigger place than I realized."

"So do you believe me now?"

"..."

Eugene's eyes narrowed, and he was silent for a moment.

One of the front lancers surrounding the terrace strode forward. He came to a halt, armor clanking, and raised the visor of his helm.

The boorish-faced man gave Eugene a salute.

"A word, Gene?"

"What is it, Kagemune?"

The name struck Leafa as familiar, and she quickly remembered. The surviving mage had mentioned it after their battle on the underground lake. Which meant he was the leader of the salamanders who'd attacked her in the Ancient Forest yesterday, during her first meeting with Kirito.

"I'm sure you're aware that my party was wiped out yesterday."

Leafa held her breath and listened closely, realizing that he was bringing up that very incident.

"Yes."

"Well, it was that exact spriggan who did it—and there was indeed an undine with him."

"…?!"

Leafa stared openly at Kagemune. Kirito's brows twitched for an instant, but he returned to his usual poker face just as quickly. Kagemune continued.

"Word from S was that he was the mage team's target as well. They didn't have much success, either."

S was most likely short for "spy." Either that or shorthand for "Sigurd."

Eugene gave Kagemune a perplexed look. No doubt the others around them were totally mystified by their conversation, but Leafa was following every word with bated breath.

Eventually, Eugene nodded. "I see." A slight grin cracked his lips. "We'll leave it at that, then."

Next, he turned to Kirito. "At the present moment, neither I nor our lord wish to get into any funny business with the spriggans or undines. We will withdraw for now—but I will have my revenge match with you."

"Looking forward to it."

Eugene cracked knuckles with Kirito's extended fist and turned away. He spread his wings and leaped into the air.

Kagemune joined him, but before doing so, he turned to Leafa and gave her a clumsy wink and smile. She took the gesture to mean that his debt was repaid. Her right cheek dimpled with a grin of her own.

Only when the two men had flown off did Leafa finally exhale the breath she'd been holding in.

As the party of dignitaries watched, the salamanders neatly resumed their battle formation and flew off with the heavy buzz of wings, Eugene at the lead. The swarm of black shapes plunged into the clouds, grew indistinct, and vanished.

With the area quiet again, Kirito said jovially, "See? Those salamanders aren't so bad after all."

Leafa didn't know what to say for several seconds. Eventually, the words bubbled up from her gut.

"...You are seriously insane."

"I get that a lot."

"...Hee-hee."

They laughed until Sakuya reminded them of her presence with a polite cough.

"Excuse me...can someone explain what is going on?"

With the meeting back to its quiet stateliness, Leafa began to explain the chain of events, clarifying that some of it was merely conjecture. Sakuya, Alicia, and the other dignitaries listened patiently and quietly. When she finally finished her explanation, they all exhaled deeply together.

"...I see," Sakuya murmured, arms crossed, a slight arch to her graceful eyebrows. "I noticed something impatient and cross about Sigurd's attitude the last several months. Wishing to rule through councils and conferences rather than tyranny, I let him take an important position in my cabinet...and it seems we've paid the price for that mistake."

"I know how hard it can be, Sakuya. You're a very popular ruler," said Alicia Rue, who'd actually been in power over her own people for longer than her sylph counterpart.

"But...what would he be so angry about?" Leafa asked curiously. Sakuya looked to the horizon as she answered.

"I suspect...that he couldn't stand for us to cede so much power to the salamanders."

" ... "

"Sigurd is a man with a strong will to power. Not just in his character's statistics but in his control over other players. No doubt he could not stand the vision of a future in which the salamanders had completed the main quest and ruled the skies of Alfheim, while he could only watch from the ground."

"But... why would he act as a salamander spy?"

"Have you heard about the upcoming update 5.0? It's rumored that they'll be implementing a reincarnation system."

"Oh... Meaning..."

"Mortimer probably put the idea in his head. He'd say, 'Take down your leader for me, and I'll let you be a salamander.' But the reincarnation process requires a vast amount of yrd, apparently. There's no saying whether Mortimer, savvy as he is, would have kept his promise, anyway."

" ... "

Leafa looked at the goldening sky and the distant haze of the World Tree, conflicted.

It was her dream to be reborn as an alf, free from the shackles of the game's flight limits. It was for that purpose that she'd joined Sigurd's party, comprised of only the strongest sylphs, and donated nearly all of the yrd she earned to the government.

If she hadn't met Kirito and left the party, it seemed likely that Sigurd would have invited her to take part in the salamander reincarnation plot. What would she have done...?

"ALO's a nasty game, testing its players' greed like this," Kirito murmured forlornly at her side. "I'm guessing its designer is a real piece of work."

"Ha. I agree," said Sakuya.

Leafa decided to follow her heart just a bit, putting her arm around Kirito's and leaning slightly into him. Kirito never seemed to be fazed by anything; being so close to him made her feel grounded and calm again.

"So... what's the plan, Sakuya?"

The smile disappeared from the beautiful politician's face, and she closed her eyes for a moment. When she opened them again, the deep green irises gleamed with a sharp light.

"Rue, you've been working on your dark magic, right?"

Alicia Rue's ears waggled in affirmation.

"Cast Moonlight Mirror on Sigurd, then."

"Sure, but it won't last long during the day."

"Not a problem. This will be brief."

Alicia's ears twitched again, and she took a step back to raise her hands and chant the spell. Her high-pitched, clear voice enunciated the unfamiliar sounds of dark magic spellwords. There was a sudden darkness around them, and a beam of moonlight shone down from somewhere.

The moonbeam piled up in front of Alicia like some golden liquid until it formed the shape of a perfectly circular mirror. As the entire gathering watched silently, the surface rippled—and a picture began to bloom within it.

"Ah…" Leafa couldn't hold in her voice. It was a familiar place to her: the meeting room of Sakuya's mansion where official business transpired.

There was a large jade-green table in front. Behind it, someone was seated in the lord's chair, his feet propped up on top of the table, his eyes closed and hands clasped behind his head. It was Sigurd.

Sakuya approached the mirror and spoke, her voice as clear as a harp.

"Sigurd."

The image of Sigurd in the mirror leaped up like a spring, his eyes wide. He must have been able to see her in return, because he looked back directly into her eyes, his mouth tense.

"S…Sakuya…?"

"That's right, still alive. Sorry to disappoint you," she replied curtly.

"Why…? I mean, what about the meeting…?"

"It will end safely. We're just about to make it official. But before that, we did have some unexpected guests."

"G-guests...?"

"General Eugene sends his regards."

"Wha—"

Now Sigurd was visibly shocked. His imposing face was going paler and paler, and his eyes swiveled as he searched for the right words. Suddenly, he caught sight of Leafa, standing behind Sakuya.

"Leaf—?!"

His eyes looked ready to pop out of his head—he'd finally grasped the situation. His nose wrinkled in anger, and he bared his teeth in a snarl.

"Incompetent lizards... Well? What's it going to be, Sakuya? A hefty fine? Expulsion from the council? Just remember, I'm in charge of our military, so you won't last long without me—"

"No. If being a sylph is so distasteful to you, I will grant your desire."

"Wh-what?"

She waved her left hand elegantly, calling up the extra-large system menu reserved for the lord of each race. Countless individual windows stacked up in layers to form a hexagonal pillar of light. She pulled out a specific tab and ran her fingers over it.

As Sigurd watched through the mirror, she called up a blue message window. Once he saw what she was doing, he stood up in a panic.

"No! Have you lost your mind?! You're... you're going to exile me?!"

"That is correct. You may wander the neutral lands as a renegade. I hope you will find new pleasures there that suit you better."

"I... I'll launch a complaint! I'll petition the GMs! This is abuse of privilege!"

"Do as you wish. Farewell, Sigurd."

He clenched his fists and prepared to launch into another tirade. But the instant Sakuya pressed the button on her tab, he disappeared from the image in the mirror. He'd been expelled from sylph land, sent randomly to any one of the neutral cities in the game aside from Alne.

The golden mirror continued to show the empty council room for a few moments, then its surface rippled again and tinkled into dust. As it vanished, the late-afternoon sun reappeared to light the area.

"Sakuya," Leafa quietly murmured into the silence, as the sylph lady's brows furrowed in thought.

The beautiful leader of the sylphs closed the game window with a swipe of her hand, then sighed and smiled.

"I suppose the next election will tell me if my decision was wise or poor. But in any case—thank you, Leafa. After all the times you refused to join the council, it makes me very happy to see you rush to our aid. Alicia, I apologize for exposing you to danger through our own infighting."

"We're alive, and that's all that matters!" the cait sith leader said perkily. Leafa hastily downplayed her part in the events.

"I didn't do anything, really. It's Kirito here who deserves your thanks."

"Ah, yes, of course. And what is your story…?"

Sakuya and Alicia Rue turned quizzical glances at Kirito.

"Hey, you. Was that true about being an envoy of the spriggans and undines?" Alicia asked, her tail waving back and forth with curiosity. Kirito put a hand on his hip and puffed out his chest.

"Complete poppycock. A bluff, a feint, a piece of negotiation."

"Wha…"

They stared at him, mouths agape.

"You're a madman. Lying through your teeth in a situation with stakes that high?"

"That's my style. When my cards are bad, I raise my bet," he said confidently. Alicia Rue flashed a mischievous feline grin and sidled over to get a better look at him.

"You're very strong for such a liar, though, aren't you? Did you know that Eugene is considered the most powerful warrior in

ALO? And you beat him in a fair fight... What are you, the spriggans' secret weapon?"

"Hardly. Just a wandering sword-for-hire."

"*Pfft!* Nya-ha-ha-ha!"

Entertained by Kirito's sass, Alicia laughed and grabbed his
right arm, squeezing it to her chest. She threw him a coquettish
glance out of the corner of her eye and purred, "If you're available, would you like to work as a mercenary for the cait siths? I
can guarantee you three meals a day, plus an afternoon nap."

"Wha..."

Leafa's mouth twitched. But before she could insert herself into
the situation—

"Now now, Rue, no cutting in line," Sakuya said, her voice even
more seductive than usual. Her long kimono sleeve wrapped
around Kirito's left arm. "He came to the sylphs' rescue, so we
have the right to negotiate with him first. Kirito, you said your
name was? I've taken a shine to you—how would you like to
share a drink back in Swilvane?"

Crik-crack. Leafa's temples were twitching now.

"Hey, no fair, Sakuya! No seducing allowed!"

"What do you call what *you're* doing? Stop rubbing yourself all
over him!"

Pulled on each side by a beautiful lady, Kirito's face went red
with embarrassment, but he didn't seem to mind too much.

Leafa had seen enough. She grabbed Kirito's cloak from behind
and pulled.

"You can't! Kirito is my..."

They all turned to look at her. Her words trailed off as she came
to her senses. "Umm...he's my..."

Unable to finish her sentence, she began mumbling, but Kirito
simply smiled and picked up the slack for her.

"I appreciate your offers, but I'm sorry—she promised to take
me to the center of the map."

"Ah, I see...That is too bad." Sakuya was not one to display

her inner feelings, but she did truly seem disappointed now. She turned to Leafa. "You are going to Alne? For recreational purposes? Or…"

"I was planning to leave the territory. But I'm sure I'll be back to Swilvane…I just don't know when."

"That is a relief to hear. Promise you'll come back—with him."

"And stop by our place on the way. You're welcome anytime!"

The two ladies pulled back and straightened up. Sakuya put a hand on her chest and tilted her head forward regally, while Alicia bowed deeply and flattened out her ears. When the courtesy was finished, Sakuya spoke again.

"Thank you once again, Leafa and Kirito. If we'd been defeated today, the salamanders' victory would have been all but guaranteed. I wish I could show my appreciation somehow…"

"There's no need," Kirito said awkwardly. Leafa suddenly realized something. She took a step forward.

"Sakuya, Alicia…this alliance is for the purpose of conquering the World Tree, isn't it?"

"Well, ultimately, yes. If we work together to scale the tree, and we both become alfs, splendid. If only one race does, they'll help the other beat the next major questline. That's the gist of the arrangement."

"We'd like to take part in the attempt. As soon as possible, actually."

Sakuya and Alicia shared a look.

"…We don't have a problem with that. In fact, we'd like you to join us. I can't make any guarantees as to a timeframe, however. Why?"

"…"

Leafa glanced at Kirito. The enigmatic spriggan boy looked down and spoke. "I came to this world because I wanted to reach the top of the World Tree. I need to meet someone who might be up there…"

"Someone? The fairy king, Oberon?"

"No...I don't think so. It's someone I can't reach in real life... but I have to find."

"So if he or she is on top of the World Tree, does that mean it's an admin? Wow, kinda mysterious, huh?" Alicia raved, her eyes sparkling. But that excitement quickly turned to dejection, her ears and tail drooping. "But...it's going to take a while to get everyone properly outfitted for the quest. It's not something that can be done in a day or two..."

"I see...good point. Then again, I just wanted to get to the foot of the tree, that's all. I'll figure out the rest on my own."

He smiled and, as though just remembering something, abruptly waved his hand to call up the menu. When he was done fiddling with his inventory, a large leather sack appeared.

"Go ahead and use this to help pay for stuff."

The sack clanked heavily—it appeared to be stuffed full of yrd. Alicia accepted it from Kirito and immediately stumbled under its weight. She shifted her hands to get a better grip and peered inside. Her eyes went wide.

"S-Sakuya, look..."

"Hmm?"

Sakuya followed Alicia's finger and peered inside. She pulled out a large pale blue coin that sparkled in the light.

"Wow..."

Leafa couldn't contain herself. The two leaders were frozen with their mouths open, and the twelve dignitaries who'd been dutifully watching the scene began to murmur excitedly.

"A hundred-thousand-yrd mithril coins...? Are these *all*—?!"

Even Sakuya was hoarse with astonishment as she examined the coin closely. She eventually put it back into the sack, shaking her head in disbelief. "You can't make this kind of money without camping out to hunt Deviant Gods in Jotunheim...Are you sure about this? You could build yourself a castle in a prime location with a sum like this."

"It's fine. I don't need it anymore," he said, unconcerned.

Sakuya and Alicia looked back into the bag and sighed deeply.

"This will put us *much* closer to the total we need."

"We'll procure equipment on the double and inform you when the preparations are complete."

"I'll be waiting."

Alicia put the leather sack into Sakuya's open inventory window.

"I won't feel safe ferrying around a gold mine like this out in the open...Let's head back to cait sith land before the 'manders change their minds."

"Good idea. We can finish the negotiations once we're safe."

The two women gave orders to their subordinates. In moments, the large table and fourteen chairs were all stowed away.

"You've helped us in every way imaginable. I promise we'll do everything we can to assist you, Kirito and Leafa."

"I'm just happy to be of service."

"We'll be awaiting your word."

Sakuya, Alicia, Kirito, and Leafa all exchanged firm handshakes.

"Thanks! See you later!" Alicia chirped with another naughty grin and pulled Kirito closer with her tail. She brushed his cheek lightly with her lips, much to his embarrassment, and flashed the twitching Leafa an enigmatic wink before spreading her pale golden wings.

The two noble ladies rose straight into the air, waving goodbye, and headed west into the reddening sky. Each was soon followed by her six compatriots in elegant formation, like flocks of geese.

Kirito and Leafa watched them go silently until they disappeared into the sunset.

The area was so quiet that the incredible duel, and the standoff in which the fate of three races hung in the balance, might as well have never happened. Only the whistling of the wind and the rustling of leaves could be heard. Leafa felt a bit chilly and leaned close to Kirito.

"...They're gone."

"Yep. It's over now…"

The schism with Sigurd that had kicked the entire string of events into motion seemed like ancient history now. She could hardly believe that it had all happened in the last seven or eight hours.

"Somehow…"

Being here with Kirito made this world feel real, as though the version of herself with wings was her real body, Leafa/Suguha thought, but she couldn't put it into words to speak aloud. Instead, she leaned against Kirito's chest, hoping to hear his heartbeat.

"I told you not to cheat on her, Papa!"

"Ah!"

Leafa leaped away as a furious Yui shot out of Kirito's chest pocket.

"Wh-what's the big idea?" Kirito moaned, as Yui circled around his head. She landed on his shoulder and puffed out her cheeks adorably.

"Your heart was racing when the royal ladies were touching you!"

"I-I can't help that; I'm a guy!!"

Leafa was momentarily relieved when she realized she wasn't the root of the problem, but a new question popped into her head, which she asked Yui.

"Um, Yui, am I allowed to…?"

"You seem to be safe, Leafa."

"W-why is that?"

"I dunno, you just don't seem all that girly to me," Kirito admitted.

"Wha— I— What's that supposed to mean?!" Leafa put her hand on her sword hilt at this unforgivable affront.

"I-I just meant you're easy to get along with…in a *good* way." Kirito laughed awkwardly, rising into the air. "C-c'mon, let's get flying to Alne! The sun's almost down!"

"Hey! Get back here!" Leafa spread her wings and leaped.

As she buzzed her wings to chase after Kirito, speeding toward the World Tree at top velocity, Leafa glanced over her shoulder. The Ancient Forest and her sylph homeland were out of sight, beyond the looming mountains, but she did catch a glimpse of a large star, twinkling in the deepening gloom of the navy sky.

—◦◦◦—

The sun, seemingly frozen in place at the very apex of the sky, did eventually fall to Earth, dyeing the curve of the horizon a brilliant red.

Asuna quietly got to her feet, calculating that at least five hours had passed in real time since Oberon's last visit. It was probably past midnight. She rolled off the bed and stepped onto the tile, praying that no one was monitoring her.

Just ten steps took her to the golden door. It was appalling to think that she'd been trapped in this cramped space for more than two months.

But that ends today, she told herself, reaching a thumb out to the ID pad next to the door. Five hours earlier, she'd watched Oberon enter the code through the mirror. She spoke each number aloud as she punched them in. The buttons had a tactile click to them, each push agitating her strained nerves.

"...3...2...9."

As she hit the last button, silently praying, there was a louder metallic sound, and the door opened just a crack. She pulled her arm back and pumped her fist in triumph, then laughed when she realized she'd picked that up from Kirito.

"Kirito...I'll do my best," she murmured, and then pushed open the door. On the other side was a winding walkway carved into the branch, which connected to the enormous trunk of the tree in the far distance. She took a step outside the cage, then another, and heard the door close automatically behind her. Asuna shook her hair back, puffed out her chest in resolution, and strode forward purposefully, the way she had once done in a different world.

A few minutes later, she turned back and saw that the golden birdcage was already lost behind the thick green foliage of the tree's branches.

She stopped about halfway down the enormous branch and caught her breath. She'd walked at least a few hundred yards by now. Its size eclipsed her imagination.

Asuna had figured, knowing Oberon's punctual, impatient nature, that he'd have set up a system console not far from the cage for the purpose of logging out. But this was not the case. If he was using an SAO-style holo-window or voice operations, her escape would be much more difficult.

She wasn't turning back, of course. She just had to go as far as she could.

I won't stop. I'm getting back to the real world, alive. I have to see him again, she swore to herself, and then resumed her march.

(to be continued)

AFTERWORD

It's good to see you again. I'm Kawahara, the author. Thank you for reading.

Let's start with my traditional list of apologies...

Just like *Accel World 3* before this, *Sword Art Online 3* ends with a dreaded "to be continued." I'm sorry!

Also, yet another new heroine has appeared in the story. Again, I'm very sorry about this. I'm afraid you might be getting very weary of this process, but...it's probably going to keep happening...Now that I think about it, *Accel* is working very much the same way. I'm not doing this intentionally—I swear. I just don't have the skill to tell a story with a variety of viewpoints, so every female character I introduce must have some kind of relationship to the protagonist out of necessity.

...Okay, I'm sorry. Forty percent of the reason is just because I like stories like that...

SAO 3 will be the final book I release in 2009. Just as I'm writing this afterword, they announced the winners of the sixteenth Dengeki Novel Prize. *It's already been a year?* I thought.

When I attended the award ceremony for last year's prize, I remember being so overwhelmed by the writerly aura emanating from all the veteran writers in attendance that I failed miserably at paying my respects. Actually, that hasn't changed; I still freeze up and work my mouth silently whenever I pass a senior writer at the editorial office.

I don't think I'll have that aura any time soon, but I *can* say that the reason I've been allowed to keep publishing books is thanks to the support of my readers. Just thinking about next year and beyond makes my head dizzy, but I hope to keep tapping away at my keyboard, working my way up this fantastically long Dengeki hill.

Again, I must extend heartfelt thanks to my incredible illustrator, abec, who has brought the pile of new characters (mostly female) to life with her usual charm! And to my editor, Mr. Miki, who had to put up with my Deadline Forgetting skill (auto-activating) when I was swamped with my event schedule, I'm so sorry!

But my last thanks of the year goes to you, for reading this book.

Hope to see you again in 2010!

Reki Kawahara—October 1st, 2009